# *The Case of the Vanishing Veil*

Bess signaled Nancy from across the street, but Nancy's mind was spinning with the shocking revelation about the veil. She didn't notice the tall blond man coming right up behind her.

Nancy started to cross the street, weaving through the traffic until she reached the yellow line in the middle. Suddenly two hands grabbed her from behind, locking her arms tightly against her sides.

She turned her head and looked straight into the glaring face of the blond man. The sun glinted off his diamond earring.

"Let me help you across the street," he said, forcing her quickly, roughly toward his car. "Don't you know you can get hurt jaywalking?"

# Nancy Drew
# Mystery Stories

## Available from MINSTREL Books

# THE CASE OF THE VANISHING VEIL

# NANCY DREW®

## 83

## CAROLYN KEENE

A
MINSTREL®
BOOK

Published by POCKET BOOKS
New York   London   Toronto   Sydney   Singapore

A MINSTREL PAPERBACK *ORIGINAL*

 A Minstrel Book published by
POCKET BOOKS, a division of Simon & Schuster, Inc.
1230 Avenue of the Americas, New York, NY 10020

Copyright © 1988 by Simon & Schuster, Inc.
Produced by Mega-Books of New York, Inc.

ISBN: 0-7434-2344-5

First Minstrel Books printing May 1988

10 9 8 7 6 5 4 3 2

Front cover illustration by Frank Sofo

Printed in the U.S.A.

# Contents

# THE CASE OF THE VANISHING VEIL

# 1

## The Veil Disappears

"It's gone. We can't find it anywhere and Meredith is hysterical," George Fayne said to her friend Nancy Drew. George was a little out of breath, and she was whispering so no one else in the beautiful old stone church could hear her. The smell of fresh-cut flowers was everywhere.

Eighteen-year-old Nancy Drew pushed back her reddish blond hair. She turned in her pew and looked at George, who was standing in the aisle beside her.

"What's gone?" Nancy whispered back.

"Meredith's wedding veil," said George. "It's an antique, and she refuses to get married without it."

"Are you sure it's not just a case of pre-wedding nerves?" asked Nancy.

"I don't know," George answered, glancing toward the back of the church. "Oh—wait a sec. Someone's motioning to me. Maybe they found it."

George picked up the skirt of her long, apricot-colored bridesmaid's dress and hurried down the aisle toward the door.

Nancy watched George leave and then swiveled back toward her friend Bess Marvin, who was sitting on the bench next to Nancy.

"What should we do?" Nancy said with an uncertain expression on her face.

"Don't look at *me*," Bess said. "*I* didn't take the bride's veil. I'm just sitting here like a good wedding guest . . . waiting patiently. I mean, am I complaining because the wedding is half an hour late, and we've come all the way to Boston for a wedding where we don't even know the bride or groom, and the church is stuffy, and my new heels are killing me? No. I'm focused on one thing and one thing only—"

"Catching the bridal bouquet," Nancy said.

"Right," Bess said.

Nancy looked at her watch for the tenth time in ten minutes. "Still, don't you think we should go help them find it?" she said to Bess. "It's getting late."

"Find the bouquet?" Bess answered.

"No, silly! The veil!" Nancy laughed. "You really *are* focused on only one thing."

"Don't worry about the veil," Bess replied. "It'll turn up. Weddings never start on time anyway."

The organist was playing the same three songs over and over. Wedding guests talked and shifted restlessly on the benches.

Nancy smoothed the skirt of her flowered print dress and listened to the conversations going on around her.

"Meredith won't be the first bride to get cold feet," a woman in front of her said.

Across the aisle two men were talking intently. "It's amazing," Nancy heard one of them say. "I read in the paper that they still haven't found an heir to the Thorndike fortune. Sixty million dollars!" He shook his head slowly back and forth.

"Mommy, I have to go to the bathroom," said a little boy in a loud voice. His mother sighed, but everyone else laughed.

"You friends of the bride?" asked a man next to Bess. He was sitting uncomfortably in a tuxedo with his hands on his knees. His wife and daughters were beside him.

"No, we're friends of George Fayne—one of the bridesmaids," Nancy said.

"George is my cousin," Bess said, plucking an invisible piece of lint from her navy blue dress. "George and Meredith met at camp and have been friends ever since," she explained.

The man's wife looked confused. "Isn't he going to feel silly being a bridesmaid?" she asked.

"George is a *girl*," Bess said coldly. She was going to say more but stopped herself when she saw George rushing back down the aisle.

"What's going on?" Bess asked when George reached the pew.

George just shook her head and said quickly, "Don't ask—follow me."

"Let's go," Nancy said, picking up her handbag and straw hat.

The three girls were quiet until they reached the vestibule of the church. Then George began speaking as she led the way up some stairs. "I was hoping everything would go perfectly for Meredith. She deserves it," George said in a serious voice. "She hasn't exactly gotten all the breaks. I mean it's awful how both her parents were killed in a plane crash when she was only eight."

"I know what that's like," Nancy said. For a moment, Nancy thought of her own mother, who had died when Nancy was three.

"Yes," George said sympathetically. "Anyway, Meredith is freaking out about her wedding veil. So I told her you were a detective and that maybe you could help."

By then they were standing outside a carved wooden door on the second floor of the church. George knocked once and opened the door.

The room was small but bright with sunlight pouring through two windows. The largest piece of furniture in the room was a full-length mirror.

Meredith Brody was sitting alone on a metal folding chair when Nancy, George, and Bess came in. She had long black hair and skin even paler than her pearl-embroidered wedding dress.

"Meredith, this is my cousin Bess and my friend Nancy Drew," George said.

The twenty-year-old bride stood up and walked forward to shake hands with Bess first.

4

"So you're George's cousin. I'm so happy to meet you at last. You're even prettier than she said." Meredith's manners were perfect, but her voice was filled with tension. Then she greeted Nancy. "Thank you for coming to my wedding. George always told me what a fabulous detective you are. But I never thought I'd need a detective on my wedding day."

"At least the groom's not missing," Nancy said warmly. "I saw him downstairs. He looks nice."

"Mark's the greatest," Meredith said, her face lighting up at the mention of her fiancé, Mark Webb. But a moment later the tension returned.

"Tell me about your veil," Nancy said. "Is it valuable?"

"No, but it's my grandmother's veil, the one she got married in," Meredith answered. "After my parents died, my grandmother brought me up. She's practically my only family. That's why it's so important to me."

Meredith ran her fingers through her long hair and started pacing around the room. "I've got to find it, and soon. Everyone down there must be wondering what's going on," she said nervously. "Maybe it blew out the window when my back was turned."

"It didn't blow out the window," Nancy said, her eyes darting around the room. "It's too far from the window to that small chest of drawers."

"How did you know I put the veil on the chest of drawers?" Meredith asked.

"There's no other place in this room to put anything," Nancy said. "Besides, that's where your hair combs are. You'd keep them nearby."

Meredith's face seemed to relax a little. "George was certainly right about you. You *are* a fabulous detective."

"Is there anyone else who knows how much the veil means to you?" Nancy asked. "Someone who might want to play a trick on you—a very cruel trick?"

Meredith shook her head no. "Honestly, I don't think I have a single enemy. I can't explain it. One minute my veil was right there and the next minute it was gone."

"What were you doing before you noticed the veil was missing?" Nancy asked.

"Well, by that time everyone in the wedding party except George had gone downstairs. I was standing at the mirror adjusting my dress, and someone knocked on the door," Meredith said. "There in the doorway was a woman with red hair and a lot of makeup. Her face was all smiles. Just looking at her made me feel good—as though she thought I was the most beautiful bride on earth. She introduced herself as Mrs. Petry, the minister's wife. She said Reverend Petry had to see me right away. So I went with her."

"Where?" Nancy asked.

Meredith walked quickly out of the small room and into the dark, narrow hallway. George, Bess, and Nancy followed, their high heels clicking on the stone floor.

At the end of the hallway, Meredith stopped in front of a solid wooden door.

"She said her husband was waiting in his office for me," Meredith said. "Go on in, Nancy. You don't have to knock."

Nancy reached for the smooth brass door handle and opened the door. Inside, a single bare lightbulb swung back and forth. It took a few seconds for Nancy's eyes to adjust to the dimness. But when they did, she saw nothing but brooms, mops, and buckets sitting on the floor.

"Gee," said Bess, "you'd think a minister would have a better office than this."

"It's a broom closet, Bess," said George.

Bess coughed.

"What did Mrs. Petry say after you opened the door?" Nancy asked Meredith.

"I turned around and she was gone."

"All right," Nancy said, turning to Bess. "Could you go find Mrs. Petry? And George, you go tell the minister that Meredith needs ten more minutes before the wedding can start."

Bess and George hurried off to find the minister and his wife, leaving Nancy alone with the unhappy bride.

"Cheer up," Nancy said kindly to Meredith. "You look absolutely beautiful—veil or no veil."

"You don't understand," Meredith said. "I *have* to get it back." She looked around in the hallway. "Maybe I carried the veil with me when I came into the hall, and then dropped it somewhere."

"That's not what happened," Nancy said. "You didn't lose the veil. Someone stole it."

Meredith let out her breath in a sigh. "That's what I think, too. But how? Besides, the minister's wife—a thief? It doesn't make sense."

"We'll see," Nancy said. "Let's reenact what happened. I'll turn around and open the door to the broom closet again. This time, you try to go back to the dressing room."

Nancy opened the closet again and stared at the cleaning tools for a moment. "Stop!" Nancy shouted, and Meredith's footsteps stopped.

Nancy turned around. "I looked inside and realized there was some kind of mistake, just as you did. So I turned around to ask Mrs. Petry what was going on, just as you did. But you said she was already gone."

"She was, and I'm only halfway down the hall," Meredith said.

"Right," Nancy answered, "which means she must have exited somewhere between here and the dressing room. She couldn't have made it all the way back there to steal the veil."

"So Mrs. Petry is innocent," Meredith said, relaxing against the wall. "I'm glad. It would have been embarrassing to tell Reverend Petry thanks for a wonderful wedding and by the way, your wife's a thief."

Both young women laughed and walked back into the dressing room.

"No, Mrs. Petry didn't steal it," Nancy said. "But I think she tricked you into leaving the room—so that someone else *could*."

Meredith's face suddenly collapsed. "I was afraid of this. It's coming true. The prediction is coming true—and my whole marriage is going to be ruined!"

She fell back onto the folding chair, and after one last brave moment, burst into tears.

Nancy opened her handbag and pulled out a handful of tissues.

"The bride's not supposed to cry at the wedding," she said. She handed all but one of the tissues to Meredith. "Here. I'm keeping one for myself—to use *during* the ceremony. Now come on and tell me what this is all about."

Meredith dried her eyes and gave Nancy a small smile.

"What a good friend you are," Meredith said. "And you don't really even know me." Then she blew her nose a few times and began talking.

"It's about a prediction," Meredith said. "You see, about a year ago, I was really down. Nothing was going right for me. So just for fun, I went to see an astrologer—Helga Tarback. She told me a lot of things about myself—all her predictions came true. Then she said I'd meet a man who had dark, angry eyes, but that I shouldn't be afraid of him because I was going to marry him."

9

"Mark Webb, your fiancé, has dark eyes," Nancy said. "In fact his eyes are riveting—I noticed."

"Right. Well, two days after I talked to Helga, I rear-ended a green sports car in a parking lot," Meredith went on. "The driver—who was Mark —jumped out, ran over, and began yelling at me. But then we looked at each other and, believe it or not, it was love at first sight. That was a year ago."

"And you went back to see Helga Tarback again?" asked Nancy.

"Yes, about three or four times," Meredith said. "Because she always told me good things, and everything she said seemed to come true. But the last time I saw her, she said she had bad news. She said that something was going to be lost or stolen on my wedding day, and if I didn't get it back, my whole marriage would be shrouded in a cloud of bad luck. Those were her exact words—'a cloud of bad luck.'"

Before Nancy could speak again, Bess and George walked back into the room.

"I couldn't find Mrs. Petry," Bess said. "But George found Reverend Petry, and wait till you hear what he said."

Nancy waited. George didn't speak up.

"Well? What did Reverend Petry say, George?" Nancy asked.

George bit her lip. "He said he's not married, and he never has been!"

Just then a car horn blasted from the street

10

below. It played "Here Comes the Bride" three times loudly. But the horn was only half as loud as the rough voice that called out afterward.

"Meredith! Meredith Brody!" shouted a young man at the top of his lungs.

Suddenly Meredith jumped to her feet and looked out the window. "Oh, no," she said, backing as far away from the window as possible. "I *knew* he'd ruin my wedding!"

"Meredith!" he shouted again. "Are you listening, sweetheart? I told you I'd be back!"

# 2

## Visitor from the Past

Meredith opened her mouth to say something, but only a small sob came out.

Nancy rushed to the window and looked down at the street in front of the church. A young man was standing on the roof of a car with his hands on his hips. "Meredith, you can run but you can't hide," he shouted.

"Who is he?" asked Nancy.

"His name is Tony Fiske," Meredith answered, anger flushing her cheeks. "And I'm sorry to admit it, but he was my boyfriend once upon a time."

"We all make mistakes," George said dryly.

"Well, my mistake with Tony was thinking that he'd outgrow talking loudly, running stop lights, and getting into fist fights. Eventually I realized what a jerk he was and told him I never wanted to see him again. But he kept trying to see me— even after Mark and I were engaged. A week ago he even had the nerve to call up to say he wouldn't let me marry anyone else."

"So you *do* have an enemy," Nancy said. "Why didn't you tell me?"

"I don't think of him as an enemy. He's just a huge mistake in my life, and I wish he would disappear."

Bess glanced at Nancy. "I'll bet Tony Fiske stole the veil," she announced. "What do you think, Nancy?"

"I think I'd like to have a word with him," Nancy said, heading for the door.

"I'm coming with you," Bess said.

"You can tell him two words for me—*get lost,*" Meredith called as Nancy and Bess hurried out of the dressing room.

They ran along the hall and down the long set of steps to the main floor of the church. Nancy pushed the heavy wooden church door open, and stepped across the threshold. Outside, it took a minute for the girls' eyes to adjust to the bright sunlight, but as soon as they could see again, Nancy and Bess realized that Tony Fiske had vanished.

"Do you think he really stole the veil, Nancy?" Bess asked.

"I don't know." Nancy sighed. "Tony's gone, Mrs. Petry's gone, Meredith's veil is gone. Nothing stays in one place long enough for me to find anything out."

"And the limo's gone, too," Bess said out of the blue.

Nancy turned to her friend. "What do you

mean, Bess? The limo is parked right in front of us."

"Not that dark limo. Didn't you see that milky white stretch limo?" Bess replied. "It was parked across from the church when we arrived."

Nancy nodded.

"I noticed it because it had one of those one-word license plates on it. LICORICE. Pretty funny for an all-white car," Bess said. "I thought for sure it was Meredith and Mark's getaway car for after the wedding. But it's gone."

Why would the bride and groom's limo leave the wedding without them? Nancy wondered. It didn't make sense.

"It's a clue, isn't it?" Bess asked, following quickly behind Nancy. "I can see it written all over your face."

Nancy, lost in her own thoughts, didn't answer her friend. Instead she walked across the church lawn and stood in front of the ivy-covered wall underneath Meredith's dressing-room window.

"Meredith!" Nancy called to the second-story window.

Meredith's head leaned out.

"Your astrologer said the veil had to be found," Nancy called. "But she didn't say it had to be found *before* the wedding, did she?"

"No," Meredith called back.

"Great. Then why don't you and Mark get married before all of your guests leave and I'll find the veil afterward?"

"Good idea!" shouted Meredith.

"You're a genius," Bess said, taking Nancy's arm. "But we've got to hurry. Now that I know the bride, I want to get a better seat!"

"Okay." Nancy laughed. "But we left our bags upstairs. You get the seats and I'll be right back."

Bess headed into the church, and Nancy climbed the stone stairs once more to retrieve their handbags. But when she got to the dressing room, a tall, imperious woman stood in front of Meredith and George, blocking the doorway. Even from the back, Nancy could see that the woman was elderly. Her gray lace dress and pillbox hat were many years out of fashion. Still, she carried herself with dignity and grace.

"Merry," said the white-haired old woman, "there are over a hundred people waiting for you downstairs. What's your problem? Second thoughts? Cold feet?" The old woman thumped her cane on the floor.

"No, Grandmother Rose," Meredith said. "It's just that my veil has been stolen."

"Your veil has been stolen?"

"Grandmother, I'd like you to meet Nancy Drew. She's a friend of George's and she's been trying to find my veil for me."

"Well, where is she?" the old woman said, thumping her cane again.

"Behind you," George answered.

Meredith's grandmother turned around.

"Nancy, meet my grandmother, Rose Strauss," Meredith said.

15

Nancy held out her hand. "How do you do?" she said. "It's so nice to meet you."

Mrs. Strauss quickly shook Nancy's hand. "Nice to meet me—hmmph. Were you a counselor at that summer camp, too?"

"No," Nancy explained. "George and Meredith were counselors together and I'm a friend of George's from home. We both live in River Heights."

"Another Midwesterner," she said, shaking her head. "Well, I'm from Maine. Maybe we Yankees take some getting used to. We don't care much about being polite—just honest. Now, what's this about the veil?"

"Someone seems to be sabotaging Meredith's wedding," George said. "A mysterious woman was walking around pretending to be the minister's wife, too."

"I expect that's the minister's problem," said Rose Strauss. "And as for that veil—I never should have given it to you in the first place, Merry." -

"Why not?" Meredith asked. She sounded hurt.

"It just covers up your pretty face," Mrs. Strauss said. "Now let's get this show on the road."

Rose Strauss walked over and started brushing Meredith's hair. Then she turned her granddaughter around for a final inspection.

"There—you look perfect," Rose said. Meredith gave her grandmother a hug and then the bridal party rushed downstairs to take their places so the wedding could begin.

The ceremony was simple, short, and lovely—just what the hot and thirsty wedding guests wanted. Meredith looked radiant, even without a veil.

Afterward Nancy and Bess congratulated the newlyweds in the receiving line outside the church.

"I'm so happy and grateful to you," Meredith told Nancy. "But I still want the veil back. After Helga's prediction, I can't help it—I guess I'm just superstitious."

"Don't worry," Nancy reassured her. "I'm on the case already. Just do me one favor: Keep your eyes open at the reception and tell me if you see the redheaded woman again. Okay?"

Meredith promised that she would.

The reception was held in a beautiful hotel in Cambridge, on the banks of the Charles River. Nancy and her friends gazed at the graceful, meandering river as their cab sped across one of the many small bridges that connected Boston to the smaller, quieter Cambridge.

As soon as Nancy, Bess, and George walked into the hotel ballroom, George was whisked away to pose for photos.

"Look at this place!" Bess gasped, her head tilted back to take in the elaborate chandeliers which hung from the ceiling. Thick, plush red carpeting covered the floors, and the walls were covered in gold and white brocade wallpaper.

"I know," Nancy agreed. "And there are three other ballrooms just like this one. We passed them in the corridor."

Nancy and Bess found seats at one of the small round tables draped with white tablecloths. But Bess didn't sit down.

"I'll get us some food," Bess offered. Eating was one of Bess's favorite occupations, whatever the occasion.

While Bess was gone, Nancy looked around the room and thought about the missing veil. Was there someone among the wedding guests who might have stolen it? Nancy wondered. Was the phony minister's wife involved? Did Tony Fiske take it as a prank? Or was something else going on?

Conversations at the nearby tables snapped Nancy out of her private thoughts. The talk seemed to be divided into two topics. Either people were saying how beautiful the bride, the ceremony, and the reception were, or they were talking about Boston's famous and recently deceased multimillionaire, Brendan Thorndike. Nancy couldn't help overhearing what they said.

At the table next to her, a husband and wife were leaning close to each other.

"Just think, Betty, if I could somehow prove that I'm the only living heir of Brendan Thorndike, the old buzzard's sixty million dollars would fall right into our laps," said the husband. He took a big gulp of champagne.

"That would be great, Dirk," said his wife, smiling fondly at him. "But half of Boston is trying to pull that same scam. Besides, you *aren't* related to Brendan Thorndike."

"A small detail," Dirk said, laughing.

Nancy's attention was suddenly drawn away to the opposite end of the room. At the table where champagne punch was being served was a woman with startlingly bright red hair.

Nancy jumped up and cut through the crowds of talkers and dancers, trying to reach the table before the red-haired woman got away. Had Meredith seen the woman? Nancy wondered. No—she was busy cutting the cake. When Nancy finally reached Meredith, the bride and the groom were laughing and wiping bits of chocolate cake and white icing off their fingers.

"Meredith," Nancy said. "Look over there. Is that the red-haired woman you saw? The one who pretended to be Mrs. Petry?"

Meredith had to wait a moment for the woman across the room to turn around. When she did, Meredith laughed. "Oh, Nancy," she said. "That's Mark's aunt Pat."

Nancy shrugged and carried pieces of wedding cake away for Bess and herself. On the way she scanned the room, looking for Meredith's grandmother, Rose Strauss. Finally she found the older woman sitting at a center table, eating a plateful of mints and nuts.

"Mrs. Strauss," Nancy said, sitting down for a

moment, "I've been trying to catch you ever since we left the church. Would you mind telling me about the veil? What does it look like?"

"It's old, handmade lace," Rose said. "And it has a very large rose worked into the center of the back. It's the only thing I saved from my wedding, and now I wish I hadn't."

"Do you have any photos of it?" asked Nancy.

"No."

Her answer was curt and definite, as if to say the subject was closed. But then she went on. "I know Meredith wants you to get the veil back. But it's of no great consequence to me, and I don't give a hoot for astrologers' predictions. As far as I'm concerned, that veil will bring Merry more bad luck if she *has* it than if she doesn't. Just look at how it almost ruined her wedding."

Rose Strauss eyed Nancy sideways before saying any more.

"Meredith is already married, so do yourself a favor, young lady. Forget about the veil and just enjoy the rest of the day."

Before Nancy could say another word, Rose stood, and the band leader stepped up to the microphone. "Ladies and gentlemen, the bride and groom will lead off the first dance. Clear the floor, please."

Nancy returned to her own table and watched Meredith and Mark dance. As George and the best man, Mark's brother, joined the couple on the dance floor, Bess dropped down next to Nancy with a plateful of sandwiches.

"Great food," she said. "Try a sandwich."

The girls spent the rest of the reception sampling the food and dancing with a few of Mark's friends. Finally the band leader announced that the bride and groom would be leaving soon.

"Will everyone please gather outside the hotel to see them off?" he said.

Instantly Bess appeared at Nancy's side and whispered one word: "Bouquet."

"Don't count on it," Nancy warned her friend.

"Oh, don't worry," Bess replied. "I made a deal."

When they got outside, the sun, which had been bright earlier, was hiding behind clouds. The air felt cooler and damper. The sky threatened rain.

And as soon as Meredith and Mark stepped out of the hotel it *did* start raining. But it rained rice, not raindrops. The young couple laughed and tried to cover themselves, but the rice came from every direction. Then, with a wink, Meredith threw her bouquet into the air and directly into Bess's waiting hands.

"Invite me to your wedding!" Meredith teased Bess.

Mark and Meredith then pushed their way through the crowd and jumped into the black limo waiting at the curb. "Goodbye, Gram! Goodbye, George!" Meredith shouted and waved behind the closed, smoked-glass window of the car.

The driver started the engine and began to pull

away. But suddenly a large black cloud of smoke and an explosion burst from the back end of the car. The startled crowd jumped back, and watched in horror as the limo lunged forward onto the sidewalk—and then smashed into an iron fence!

# 3

## The White Limousine

"What happened?"

"Call the police!"

"Are they hurt?"

Everyone was shouting at once and running toward the car. Its back fender was crumpled and its front end was wedged up against the iron fence.

After a long minute, the limo driver swung his door open and climbed out. He was shaking his head, confused and dizzy. But he was uninjured. He jerked the back door open and looked in as the crowd closed around him.

"They're all right!"

The word spread quickly, but Nancy didn't feel relieved until Meredith and Mark climbed out of the car. Rose Strauss, who was standing away from the crowd with Bess, took a deep breath.

"I heard that big boom, and I just lost control," the driver explained over and over. "I just lost control."

23

When Nancy reached the car, Meredith was leaning on it, crumpling a "Just Married" sign in her hand. Mark was beside her, his arm wrapped snugly around her shoulders.

"I can't help it, Mark," she said to him. "It's true. We *are* starting our marriage under a cloud of bad luck."

Mark's dark eyes looked steadily into Meredith's, and his voice was calm. "Meredith," he said, "we don't have to cancel our honeymoon just because a couple of weird things happened."

"Do you want a life filled with accidents?" she said.

"This wasn't an accident," Nancy interrupted. "I just checked out the rear of the car. Someone put some small plastic explosives in a tin can and tied it to the bumper."

"Explosives?" Meredith said. "Oh, great!"

"It's not that serious," Nancy said. "It was just meant to make some smoke and noise. The can bouncing on the cobblestone street probably set it off."

The crowd let Rose Strauss and Bess through, and Meredith gave her grandmother a long, clinging hug.

"We're both fine, Mrs. Strauss," Mark said. "We just want to get out of here."

"Speak for yourself," Meredith said. "I don't want to go. I want my veil back so this horrible prediction won't come true."

Mark gave Nancy a pleading look, and at the

same time, Bess poked Nancy in the side. Everyone expected her to do something.

"Meredith, listen," Nancy said, mustering her most confident tone of voice. "I promised I'd find your veil and I will. Really. Go on your honeymoon, and by the time you get back, I'll have solved this case."

Meredith still hesitated.

"If anyone can do it, it's Nancy," George reassured her friend.

Meredith seemed to relax a little when she heard that.

"Okay, but I'll call you every day to find out how it's coming," Meredith said.

One of Mark's friends hailed a taxi and then transferred the luggage and the bride and groom into the cab. The guests stayed to watch the taxi bounce away down the narrow stone street, making certain Meredith and Mark were safely on their way this time.

"It was a nice wedding, even with the extra excitement, wasn't it?" George said to her friends.

"It was wonderful," Bess agreed with a sigh. "But now let's go back to our hotel and recuperate."

"Good idea," George said. "But I feel an attack of tourist-itis coming on. How about going for a sunset Swan Boat ride?"

"Not until I get out of these high heels," said Bess.

"And I want to call my dad first," Nancy said.

The three friends quickly hailed a cab and hopped in.

"To the Ritz!" Bess said to the cabdriver in her most theatrical voice.

They were staying in the famous Ritz-Carlton, one of Boston's most elegant hotels. Ordinarily, the Ritz would have been too extravagant for the three teenagers. But the hotel had a special rate for guests staying more than just a few days. By splitting it three ways, Nancy, Bess, and George could afford to indulge in a little luxury.

Nancy entered their room, which faced a beautiful park, and flopped down onto one of the brocade bedspreads covering the enormous beds. Bess kicked off her shoes and collapsed in a huge chair. And George, who was never really comfortable in a dress, immediately changed into pants.

"I'm hungry," Bess announced, heading for the room's mini-refrigerator. It was stocked with sodas and juices, nuts and candy bars.

"But you just ate at the reception!" George teased.

"That doesn't count," Bess complained. "Everyone knows that you never really get full at a buffet like that. You just keep filling those tiny little plates, and then when you get home, you still feel like you haven't had anything to eat. Where's the room-service menu?"

While Bess read the menu, George thumbed through a sightseer's guide to Boston, and Nancy called her father, Carson Drew, River Heights's most prominent attorney.

"Guess who," Nancy said into the phone.

"The Queen of England? I've always wanted to get a call from her," said Carson Drew, laughing.

"You're funny sometimes, you know that?" Nancy said.

"Thank you. I do my best. How's Boston? And how was the wedding?"

"Beautiful . . . but, Dad, I need a favor," said Nancy.

"That's strange," Carson Drew said. "You only say that when you're working on a mystery—not when you're a guest at a wedding."

"Actually, Dad, there is a mystery involved; the bride's veil was stolen."

"So you *are* working on a case," Nancy's father said with surprise. "What's the favor?"

"You've always said you have a friend in every police department across the country," Nancy began. "Who is it in Boston? I need to trace a license plate."

"No problem," said Carson Drew. "Lieutenant Burt Flood. He's an old friend."

"Thanks, Dad, I'll tell him you said hello."

After hanging up with her father, Nancy made a quick call to the police station to let the lieutenant know she was coming.

Thirty minutes later her taxi pulled up to the precinct house.

She found Lieutenant Burt Flood at his desk, surrounded by stacks and stacks of papers, files, newspapers, and memos. When he stood up to greet Nancy, he wore a big smile.

"Carson Drew's daughter? I don't believe it," the heavyset policeman said in a gravelly voice. "His little girl is three years old."

"I was three—fifteen years ago," Nancy said. She moved a stack of folders to sit down in a chair by his desk.

"Has it been fifteen years? I don't believe it," said Lieutenant Flood. "So what are you doing in Boston? Vacation?"

"I came here for a wedding, but now I'm working on a case," Nancy said. "I'm a detective."

"I don't believe it," he said again.

"My dad said you'd help me trace a license plate," Nancy went on, ignoring his skepticism.

"Well," he said, looking at her intently for a long minute. Then he broke into a broad smile. "For Carson Drew's daughter, anything. I can have that for you in just a few minutes."

The lieutenant tapped a few keys on his computer keyboard. "Okay, I'm ready. What's the plate number?"

"It's actually a one-word plate—LICORICE."

*Tap tap tap.* Lieutenant Flood squinted at the screen as he wrote down a name and address and handed it to Nancy. "Very fancy address. Lives in the Beacon Hill area," he said.

"Thanks," Nancy said.

"Any time," the policeman answered. "It was

great seeing you again. I'll bet your dad's real proud of you."

As soon as Nancy left the precinct, she opened the folded piece of paper.

It said: Cecelia Bancroft, 1523 Chestnut Street.

Nancy looked at her watch, eager to follow up this lead. But there wasn't time. She had promised to join Bess and George back at the hotel to go for a Swan Boat ride.

Well, Nancy thought to herself, a little tourist activity before starting this new case wouldn't be a bad idea. Things would get pretty intense soon enough. Her cases always did.

When she got back to the hotel, Nancy phoned her friends from the lobby telephone. A few minutes later, they were in the Boston Public Garden, a park right across the street from the Ritz. Nancy was happy to finally see the famous Swan Boats, named for their swan shape. Now, at least, when every hotel clerk and bellboy asked, "Have you been on the Swan Boats yet?" Nancy could say yes!

The three friends enjoyed the relaxing ride as they watched the beautiful green garden pass by and dusk slowly fall.

After a supper of seafood and chowder, they returned to their room and collapsed. Each girl found a comfortable spot and sat with pencil and paper, writing. George made a list of places she wanted to see in Boston. Bess made a shopping list. And Nancy sat on her bed, working on a list of suspects and clues in the stolen veil case.

"We have two suspects," Nancy said, as she began to write. "One has a name—Tony Fiske—and a very good motive. He's Meredith's old boyfriend. He's hot-tempered and he wanted to make her mad. The other suspect has red hair. She has a name, too, but we don't know what it really is."

"We *do* know that it isn't Mrs. Petry," George said, looking up from her own paper.

"And now we add Cecelia Bancroft to the list, because she owns the white limo which was parked right outside the church when the veil was stolen," Nancy said.

Nancy looked at the list for a full five minutes without saying a word.

"I think Tony is our man," she finally said to George. "But I'll see what Cecelia Bancroft has to say tomorrow."

The next morning Nancy found Tony Fiske's number in the phone book and called him several times. No one answered.

So she, Bess, and George dressed quickly and went over to Beacon Hill. It was an area famous for its beautiful old houses with wealthy, old Boston families in residence. There they found Cecelia Bancroft's house on a historic, tree-lined street.

Nancy turned the brass crank-handle doorbell,

which was in the middle of a solid wooden door. A noisy dog began barking on the other side.

The woman who opened the door was in her forties, very pretty with soft blond hair. She wore a satin jumpsuit and held a small black poodle tightly in her arms.

"Cecelia Bancroft?" asked Nancy.

"Yes," answered the woman. "If you three girls have come about the ad in the paper, I'm afraid you're too late."

Nancy shook her head no. "No, we're—" But before Nancy could say anything more, the dog started barking again.

"Oh, hush up, Licorice, hush up," Cecelia said.

"I'm Nancy Drew," Nancy said. "We haven't come about the ad in the paper, but we'd like to ask you a few questions about a robbery."

"A robbery!" the woman gasped. "Here? On Chestnut Street?"

"No," Nancy replied. "Yesterday, at the Park Road Church."

Cecelia looked puzzled, but she showed the girls into a large room. The dog followed, growling at their feet.

"You chose your license plate to go with your dog's name, didn't you?" Nancy asked, keeping an eye on the unfriendly black dog.

"Well, of course," Cecelia said. "It would be stupid to do it the other way around—name your dog after your license plate—wouldn't it? Then

you'd end up with a dog named T2485, or
something! But how do you know my license
plate?"

"We saw your car parked outside the Park
Road Church yesterday," Nancy said.

"Oh, I see," Cecelia said. "You have a miniature poodle too. Wonderful doggies, aren't
they?"

"No, we don't own a poodle," George said.

"Then what were you doing at Bruno's French
Poodle grooming shop?" asked Cecelia.

"We weren't at the poodle grooming shop,"
Nancy said. "We were at the Park Road Church
—at a wedding."

"Oh, of course. That's right across the street
from Bruno's," said Cecelia. "You know, I always cry at weddings. Of course, I always cry
when Licorice is groomed, too. That's why I
drop him off and leave as fast as I can. Who was
married?"

"My friend, Meredith Brody," George said.

"I don't know her, but I'm sure she was a lovely
bride," Cecelia answered.

Nancy looked at George. Both girls wondered
if Cecelia was putting on this airhead act to
confuse them. Nancy decided to get right to the
point.

"She would have been lovelier if she had had
her veil to wear," Nancy said.

"Did she forget it?" Cecelia asked, playing
with her dog's ears.

"It was stolen," Nancy said.

32

"A robbery—during a wedding—in a church! How unusual!"

"So you weren't at the church after all," Bess muttered. "I guess that would explain why the car disappeared."

"Sorry," Cecelia apologized, shrugging her shoulders.

"Well, I wonder if you saw anything or anyone suspicious when you were there?" Nancy said.

Cecelia shook her head, then giggled. "It's funny—you sound just like a detective."

"I know," Nancy said. "I am."

But Cecelia didn't seem to hear and went right on. "You know the same thing happened to me at my wedding only it was completely different." She put the little dog in her lap and thought for a moment. "I was so nervous, I went to the wrong church. And there was a wedding going on in there, too. So I strolled down the aisle. Can you believe it? I came this close to marrying a man I didn't even know."

Nancy decided to give up on this line of questioning.

"Well, thank you for your time anyway," Nancy said.

Nancy, Bess, and George stood up to leave, but Cecelia stayed seated.

"I've got to tell you," she said, "I feel terrible for that poor girl. I know what it's like to start off a wedding on the wrong foot."

"Thanks," Nancy said. "I'm sure we'll find the veil."

"I'm sure you will. What are you going to do next?" Cecelia asked.

"We're going back to the church," Bess said.

"Isn't there something I can do to help?"

Nancy tried to think of a polite way to decline Cecelia's offer, but she took too long.

"Now see if this doesn't sound like a good plan," Cecelia said. "I'll put on my thinking cap and try to remember anything suspicious. And if I do, I'll meet you at the church in two hours."

Cecelia showed them to the front door, talking non-stop every step of the way. "It'll take me that long to explain to Licorice why I'm going out without him. He's very protective. My husband goes off and leaves me alone every day—of course, he has a job and Licorice doesn't."

Outside, the three girls were happy to be out in the sunlight—and away from the chattering Cecelia Bancroft.

"I wonder what her thinking cap looks like," George said, giggling.

"She's very friendly, which is more than I can say for her dog," Bess said. But then she noticed that Nancy wasn't listening to her.

Nancy was giving her full attention to a figure lurking behind a lamppost across the street.

"That's Tony Fiske," Nancy said.

"You're right," George replied.

"What's he doing *here*?" Bess said.

That was exactly what Nancy wanted to know. Was he following them? Not likely. Tony didn't even know who they were. Was he there by coincidence? Or had he come to see Cecelia?

Just then, Tony moved sideways a little and looked directly at Cecelia's front steps. Nancy froze for an instant, waiting to see what he would do. He didn't seem to recognize her at all. Instead he casually lifted the lid of a heavy metal garbage can near the curb and tossed an empty soda can inside.

Nancy ran quickly down the steps and started across the street.

"Tony Fiske?" she called.

At the sound of his name, Tony stepped into the street. He waited a second—until Nancy drew closer—and then he reached behind him. With one swift motion Tony Fiske sent the trash can rolling dangerously in Nancy's path!

# 4

## *The Clue in the Church*

As a surprised Nancy tried to dodge the trash can, Tony Fiske took off, running like a rocket down the cobblestone street. She managed to sidestep the rolling can, but she tripped over the lid and fell, skinning her hands on the pavement.

By the time Bess and George reached her, Tony was at the corner of Chestnut Street, crossing the street diagonally. *He's getting away,* Nancy thought as she dashed into the street, ignoring the oncoming traffic. A car horn blared at her as its tires squealed to a stop. She gave the driver a quick backward look of apology as she ran on. But a bus had pulled up near the curb, blocking the sidewalk. When Nancy finally wove her way through the jumble of vehicles, Tony was gone.

"He got away," Nancy said. She was completely out of breath when Bess and George caught up with her.

"I wonder what he was doing here? I mean, outside Cecelia's house?" Bess asked.

"Maybe following us . . ." George suggested.

"I don't think he was following us," Nancy said. "But if he was, we'll see him again."

"And next time," George said, running her hand through her short hair, "we'll be faster."

On the way to the Park Road Church, the girls bought postcards and then stopped for a cold soda. As they drank their soft drinks, they wrote out their postcards to Nancy's boyfriend, Ned Nickerson, who was a student at Emerson College.

"Having a wonderful time. Wish you were here," wrote Nancy.

Bess wrote, "Nancy's name has been linked with a Tony Fiske. Aren't you dying?"

George's note was the shortest of all: "Don't believe Bess!"

Exactly at noon, they arrived at the Park Road Church, half expecting to see Cecelia's white stretch limo parked outside. The parking spaces were empty, however.

Yesterday, the church had been cheerful and festive for Meredith's wedding. But today it seemed as though the newlyweds had taken all the happiness with them when they left. Now the old stone church looked dark and gloomy. The stained-glass windows had been shuttered over from the inside, and so only narrow streaks of sunlight, like dusty stripes, fell across the wooden pews.

Slowly the three friends entered the church and walked from the door into the chapel.

37

"Looking for someone?" a voice asked in the dark. Footsteps approached. Then a familiar face came out of the shadows. It was Reverend Petry, the minister. He was a quiet but cheerful man in his fifties with silver hair and glasses. "I'm not really trying to create the atmosphere of Dracula's castle," he said, turning on a tall lamp that stood on the aisle. "I'm just trying to cut down on the electricity bill."

"Reverend Petry, we were here yesterday," George said, "for Meredith and Mark's wedding."

That made the minister smile. "I was afraid for a while that it wasn't going to happen," he said, grinning. "Too bad I don't get paid for overtime. Well, have you come back because you left something behind?"

"No, we came back to look for the bride's veil," Bess said.

"But I understood that my *wife* stole that," the minister teased.

"We're trying to find out who really did steal it," Nancy said.

Just then the front door opened with a bang. "Anybody home?" called out a woman's voice from the doorway.

Nancy turned. "Uh-oh, bad news," she murmured to her friends as she recognized the soft blond hair. "Cecelia Bancroft decided to show up after all."

"Hello, ladies," she said with a wave. She came forward into the aisle and held her hand out to Reverend Petry. "Hello. Cecelia Bancroft."

"Roger Petry," the minister said, shaking her hand.

"It's a tad gloomy around here, don't you think?" asked Cecelia.

Reverend Petry cleared his throat. "Well, the Sunday morning services are over," he said.

"Reverend Petry, would it be all right if we looked around the second floor of the church?" Nancy asked.

"Sure," said the minister. "Though I doubt you'll find the veil."

Nancy didn't hold out much hope for it either. In fact, she wasn't sure what she was looking for. At the very least, she hoped she might find out how the red-haired woman had disappeared so fast—and how someone had gotten in and out of the dressing room without being noticed. At most, she hoped for a clue to the thieves' identities.

Cecelia and the three girls went up the dark staircase to the second floor, and had been searching in the long, narrow hallway for only a minute when Cecelia cried out, "Look at this!" She was holding something in her hand.

"What is it?" asked Bess, who was shining a penlight on a nearby section of the hallway.

"A penny," Cecelia said. "Things are looking up." She handed it to Bess. "You can put it in the collection box."

Nancy sighed and walked back down the dark

hallway from the dressing room to the broom closet. This time she opened all the other doors along the way. Closet. Office. Storage room. Main stairway—no, door. Office. Fuse box with circuits. Another stairway. And finally the broom closet Meredith had been led to.

Nancy stepped back to the door before the broom closet.

"This is how the woman with the red hair disappeared so fast," Nancy announced. "She must have known about this other stairway. She ran down the steps while Meredith's back was turned."

"But who took the veil? And how did that person get away?" Bess asked.

"I don't know," Nancy said.

"I'll check out this other stairway," George volunteered. Cecelia went with her.

Nancy stayed in the main hallway because the beam of her flashlight had caught something in its light. She walked over to the storage closet door and stooped to pick up her discovery.

"Find something?" asked a voice behind her.

Nancy jumped.

"Bess," Nancy said, "make more noise, will you?"

"Sorry about that, Nancy," Bess said. "What is that?"

Nancy stood up and opened her palm. In it was a flower, fading and dry. "It's probably from Meredith's bouquet."

"Is that a clue?" Bess asked.

40

"I don't know," said Nancy. "I doubt it."

"Hey!" George shouted.

Nancy and Bess could hear her footsteps as she came running up the back stairway and into the hall. Cecelia followed.

"Nancy, Cecelia found something on the stairs," George said.

Cecelia held a thin, rectangular slip of paper. The three girls crowded around to read it in Nancy's flashlight.

"It's part of an airline ticket," Bess said.

Nancy was too busy reading the handwritten information on the ticket to say anything.

"The passenger's name is Markella Smith," Nancy said finally. "She flew from Denver to Boston yesterday."

"Look at that!" George said. "She arrived just three hours before Meredith's wedding."

"And she's scheduled to fly back to Denver tonight!" Nancy said. Her mind was racing. The ticket had been issued yesterday. That meant it had to be dropped there either yesterday or today.

"Let's say that Markella Smith has red hair," Nancy mused aloud. "Yesterday, she flies from Denver to Boston. She comes to this church. We know she couldn't have done this alone. So, she and her accomplice sneak up this back stairway together, and wait."

"She tricks Meredith into leaving the room," George added.

"Right," Nancy agreed. "And her accomplice

41

is already hiding in that office—down the hall."
Nancy pointed to the office near the dressing
room. "When Meredith leaves, the accomplice
sneaks into the dressing room and takes the veil.
Then he or she sneaks back into the office and
waits till the coast is clear to sneak out of the
church."

"Meanwhile, Markella Smith has already gone
down the back stairway," George added.

"But she lost a page of her ticket while she was
waiting there," Bess chimed in.

"Whew!" Cecelia Bancroft whistled. "You
girls are serious!"

"But *why*—that's the question, isn't it, Nancy?
Why would Markella Smith want to steal Meredith's wedding veil?" Bess asked.

"It's the question, all right. And it's a question
only *she* can answer," Nancy said, putting the
ticket in her jeans pocket.

"What are you going to do?" Cecelia asked.
"Fly to Denver?"

"If I have to," Nancy said. "But first I'll try
calling her."

"But that won't help," Cecelia interjected.
"Markella Smith isn't home yet. She's flying back
to Denver tonight, remember? Maybe you should
go to the airport and catch her there."

"Good idea," Nancy admitted. "Thanks for
your help, Cecelia."

"Anytime. Too bad I can't come along," Cecelia said. "My husband and I are giving a

dinner party tonight so I have to hurry home. But remember to let me know how things turn out."

Cecelia left the Park Road Church first, and after thanking Reverend Petry, Nancy, Bess, and George followed.

"Well, we don't have to be at the airport until this evening," Bess said when they were alone on the sidewalk. "Let's take a bus to Filene's Basement—and spend some cash!"

Nancy had never been to Filene's department store, but she had heard about it for weeks from Bess. As they walked through the revolving doors, Nancy saw that everything Bess had said was true. Filene's was a normal department store from the ground floor up. But in the basement there were racks and racks of famous designer clothing being sold at a fraction of the original price. The entire basement display area was packed from wall to wall with eager, shoving, no-nonsense bargain hunters.

"I think I'll wait until after the fight is over," George said, standing back by the elevator.

"They aren't fighting," Bess said. "They're shopping! Let's go!"

Bess took a deep breath and disappeared into the crowd.

With a laugh, George asked Nancy, "Think we'll ever see her again?"

A few hours after the shopping spree, they dropped their packages off at the hotel and then went to pick up the rental car Nancy had arranged for shortly after leaving the church earlier that afternoon. Soon the three friends were headed for Boston's Logan Airport. After parking their car, they checked the monitors for the number of the flight from Boston to Denver, and found that it was scheduled to depart from Gate 10. Then they settled into chairs just outside the security checkpoint to wait for Markella Smith.

The problem with this arrangement, Nancy soon realized, was that hundreds of passengers were going through security every hour. There was no way to know which ones were headed toward Gate 10 and which ones were headed toward the other nine gates in this section of the airport.

"If we could just go *through* security," Bess said, "it would be better. Then we could wait in the area right near the gate."

"Yes," Nancy agreed, "but as the sign says—"

"—only ticketed passengers are permitted beyond this point," George said, imitating the airport security people.

"We need a new plan," Nancy said.

She got up and walked back to the ticket desk.

"I'd like to find out if a passenger named Markella Smith has checked in yet," Nancy said to the woman behind the desk, whose name tag said Ms. Palomino.

"I can't give out that information," Ms. Palomino explained.

"It's very important that I talk with her," said

Nancy. "I missed her when she came in on Flight 320 yesterday morning."

"No, you didn't," answered the woman.

Ms. Palomino's remark caught Nancy by surprise, but she had a good reason for saying it. "Flight 320 was canceled yesterday," she explained. "Maybe she came in on another airline."

"Right," Nancy said.

"Anything else, miss?" asked Ms. Palomino with an edge in her voice. There was a long line of people waiting behind Nancy.

"Yes," Nancy said. "I'd like to buy a ticket to Denver. Can you give me the seat next to Markella Smith?"

Ms. Palomino sighed, but she tapped on her computer keyboard. Then she shook her head. "There isn't anyone named Markella Smith on the passenger roster. Believe it or not, there's not a single Smith listed on the flight."

"Are there any other flights to Denver?" Nancy asked.

"Not tonight," said Ms. Palomino.

George and Bess were clearly disappointed when Nancy reported that it was time to go back to the hotel.

"But we didn't learn anything," Bess exclaimed.

"This mystery seems to have fizzled out," George agreed.

"Not for me," Nancy said.

To Nancy, the fact that Markella Smith didn't

show up at the airport made the whole thing even more mysterious. Did this mean Markella Smith was still in Boston? And who *was* Markella Smith anyway? Had she been invited to the wedding? And if so, as a friend of the bride's or the groom's? Or was she a stranger—a stranger who for some reason was interested in Meredith's veil?

"Tomorrow we should find out if Markella Smith was on the guest list," Nancy said as George drove through the exit at Logan Airport.

But George wasn't paying any attention to her. Her mind was on the road.

"Nancy, it's so dark," George said. "Does it look to you like our right headlight is out?"

"Pull over and I'll check," Nancy volunteered.

"No—don't pull over," Bess said sharply. "Please, don't stop!"

By then, George was almost on the highway.

Nancy started to turn around, to find out why Bess was upset. But Bess leaned forward from the backseat and grabbed Nancy's arm so tightly that Nancy almost cried out. Nancy turned a little and looked into her friend's frightened face.

"What is it?" Nancy asked.

Bess held her breath.

"Don't look now," she whispered, "but we're not alone. We're being followed!"

# 5

# Blackout!

Nancy looked out the back window of the car.

"Who's following us?" she asked.

"Don't you see that silver car? It followed us all around the airport parking lot," Bess said. "We've got to get out of here."

George checked the rearview mirror and the side mirrors.

"Which silver car?" George said. "The one next to us, the one in front of us, or the one in back?"

"I can't tell now," said Bess. "There's too much traffic."

"Well, there's one way to find out if Bess is right," Nancy said. "Quick, George. Take the next exit."

George jerked the steering wheel to the right. Their rental car jumped from the middle lāne to the exit lane, knifing in front of several cars. Surprised drivers blasted their horns.

"Now everyone thinks I'm a lousy driver," George said.

"Maybe," Nancy said, watching a sleek silver car behind them make the same fast maneuver. "But now we know Bess is right."

"I *knew* it!" Bess said triumphantly. Then she shuddered. "At times like this, I hate to be right."

"Okay, fasten your seat belts for takeoff," George said. She stepped on the gas.

George got off the highway and made several fast turns, trying to lose the silver car behind them. Soon the girls found themselves on a narrow dirt road. Nancy glanced backward. The silver car was still behind them.

"He's pretty smart. He's got his high beams on so we can't see his face," Nancy said. "And there's no license plate on the front of the car."

"What do you bet it's Tony Fiske?" Bess said.

"I'm not making any more bets with you," Nancy said with a smile. "Besides, Tony doesn't own a car. Remember? Meredith told us yesterday in the church."

"But we don't own a car either—not in Massachusetts, anyway," Bess said. "We rented one—remember?"

"Good point," Nancy said.

Their car sped onto a dark, two-lane road that dipped and twisted. They passed small farms. George's lips were pressed tightly together, and she drove with both hands gripping the wheel.

Nancy looked back at the silver car.

"He could catch us if he wanted to. But he's

hanging back," Nancy said. "Maybe he wants to see where we're going."

"Where *are* we going?" asked Bess.

"I don't know," George said.

"What do you mean you don't know?" cried Bess. "You're the driver!"

"But I've been trying to lose this guy," George said. "I haven't been watching the road signs."

"Relax. We'll come to a sign soon," Nancy said.

"Maybe it'll say River Heights," Bess said, trying to hide her fear with a joke.

But George didn't laugh. "I hope it says *Gasoline*," she said pointedly.

Nancy and Bess looked at the needle. It registered E, for empty.

How many things could go wrong at once? Nancy thought with frustration. They were lost, traveling down a dark two-lane road. An unknown driver was following them, and they were about to run out of gas.

Just then a sign appeared announcing that the next city was only two miles away.

"Wait!" Bess said when she saw the name of the town on the sign. "Are you sure we want to go to *Salem,* Massachusetts? That's where they burned witches at the stake."

"That was three hundred years ago, Bess," Nancy replied. "Besides, we've got to find a gas station. Keep driving, George, there's bound to be one ahead."

A moment later Nancy, Bess, and George

pulled into a dark, quiet city where every store was closed up tight. The first sign they saw said Welcome to Salem, Massachusetts. To Bess's horror, there was a picture of a witch on it. The next two signs advertised the Witch Trail and the Witch House.

Except for the silver car behind them, the streets of Salem were completely deserted. They passed stores like Hilda's Broom Closet, the Cauldron Coffee Shop, and the Tisket-A-Tasket Casket Book Store, hoping to see some signs of life—a lighted window, a human being, even another car. But the town was dead.

Finally the two-car procession—their car followed by the silver one—came to the center of town. A Gothic stone building loomed like a dark giant over the town square. Even in the daytime the building would have looked forbidding. But in the dead of night, it looked absolutely gruesome.

"What is that?" asked Bess.

George read the sign. "It's the Salem Witchcraft Museum," she said.

"Why are we stopping in front of it?" Bess asked, looking out the back window. "In fact, why are we stopping at all?"

"We're out of gas," Nancy said quietly.

The silver car stopped thirty feet behind them and turned off its headlights. The waiting game began.

"Forget it!" Bess suddenly shouted. "I'm not just going to sit here." She leaped from the car and started running across the square without any idea where she was going.

Instantly Nancy and George jumped out of the car and began running after her.

"Bess! Wait!" Nancy shouted.

Nancy heard another car door slam behind her, and she knew without looking that the driver of the silver car had gotten out.

If only Bess hadn't gotten out of the car, Nancy thought to herself. At least in the car, with the doors locked, they were somewhat safe. Here, on the streets of Salem, all the shops were closed, locked, and dark. There was no place to hide or get help.

Bess turned down a side street and George ran twice as fast to catch her.

Nancy looked back. The driver of the silver car was only a block away. He was tall, Nancy could see. But in the shadows, that was the only thing about him she could make out. He was running right toward her.

She turned the corner, following George and Bess.

For the next ten minutes, the girls ran through the empty streets, turning this way and that. Every street was dark. The whole town was sleeping.

Eventually George and Nancy caught up with Bess. But the tall man pursuing them was still a block behind.

"We could split up," Nancy said, breathing heavily. "He can't chase all three of us at once."

"No!" Bess whispered. "Let's go this way."

She raced down an alley and the others followed. Tired, their legs aching and cramped, the three girls slowed to a walk. The footsteps behind them slowed, too. Halfway down the alley, they realized they had made a terrible mistake. They were in a dead end—trapped! There was no way out.

Suddenly Nancy spotted a light in the window of a tall stone building on their right. She beckoned to her friends and they followed her to the building's back door.

"Is it unlocked?" George whispered. The figure of their pursuer was a tall silhouette at the far end of the alley.

Nancy nodded. "If this creep follows us in, at least we'll be able to see him in the light," she said.

But when the girls stepped into the gloomy building, they found it dark. Apparently the light they had seen was coming from a room above. In the pitch blackness, they climbed a stone stairway leading up to a landing. There Nancy found a black curtain. She parted it to peek into a dimly lit room.

"Where are we?" Bess asked.

"Brace yourself, Bess. You aren't going to like this," Nancy said.

She stepped through the curtain and held it open so that George and Bess could follow.

The minute Bess moved forward, her skin

turned icy cold. There, a few feet away, was a young woman being burned at the stake!

"I think we're in the Witchcraft Museum," Nancy said.

"No, no, no," Bess moaned.

Just then all the lights went out and the whole building went black.

# 6

## Inside the Witchcraft Museum

In the pitch-dark museum, Nancy reached out and grabbed the shoulder closest to her. It was Bess's and she was trembling.

"He's followed us in here," George said in a whisper.

"Don't move, Bess," Nancy whispered.

"I'm too scared to move," Bess answered.

They listened in the darkness. Footsteps . . . slow footsteps . . . in another room . . . coming closer . . .

Nancy felt Bess almost collapse. "Don't scream," she told her friend.

"He can't see us in the dark," George said.

"So what?" Bess answered quickly. "We can't see how to get out of here either."

"Shhh," said Nancy.

The footsteps were in the room now.

A man's voice called out, "Who's there?"

The three girls shivered. Bess pulled away from Nancy quickly, and the next thing they heard was a loud crash. "Oh, no," Bess moaned. Then the lights snapped on.

Bess was standing by a mannequin dressed in witch's rags that was part of a display. She had run into it in the dark and sent it crashing to the floor.

Nancy looked from Bess to the young man standing in the doorway. The museum lights reflected off his long, curly brown hair. He wore a white silk dress shirt and khaki jeans, and held a long ax with both hands. The handle was longer than he was tall. Its curved blade was as big as a watermelon.

The three girls froze with fear.

"What do you want?" Bess asked in a terrified voice.

The man walked toward them, turning the ax in his hands. "You know, three hundred years ago the penalty for trespassing was having a leg cut off—and that was considered just a warning," he said with a satisfied smile. He stopped a few feet from them. Then he asked, "What are you doing in here?"

George started to answer, but she hesitated. It was difficult to take her eyes off that enormous ax.

Nancy spoke up. "Why have you been following us all night?" she demanded.

"I haven't been," said the man.

Suddenly a door down the stairs behind them slammed loudly.

Bess jumped. "What was that?"

"That was the museum's back door," the man said. His voice turned from calm to concerned. "Someone just left in a very big hurry. You *were* being followed, weren't you?"

"Yes," all three girls said at once.

"Hold this," said the man, handing the ax to George. "I'll take a look downstairs."

"And I'll come with you," Nancy said quickly.

Together the two went through the black curtain and down the stairs. The museum's ground floor was completely quiet—and completely deserted.

"Well, whoever followed you inside has left," the man said. "I'll lock the door to make sure he stays out. By the way, I'm David Kaufman, the curator of this museum."

Nancy introduced herself, and David locked the door. Back upstairs, the detective introduced him to her friends.

"I'm really sorry about knocking over your witch," said Bess.

"That's all right." David smiled. "Meredith has a worse fate planned for her future."

"Meredith!" George and Nancy both said at once.

"Yes, I must admit that I name all of my witches in the museum," David said sheepishly. "This is Meredith. She's going to be beheaded in the next exhibit."

He took the ax from George and set it down, then moved the witch mannequin over to a chopping block. "I came in tonight to set up this display for tomorrow," he explained. "Pretty realistic, don't you agree?"

The girls agreed, and then Nancy told David about being followed, about running out of gas, and finding the back door of the museum unlocked.

"Why were you being followed?" David asked somewhat suspiciously. "You're not witches, are you?" he teased.

"No—we're detectives," Nancy answered. "Or at least I am. I'm on a case for a young woman named Meredith, who lost her wedding veil."

David smiled. "Meredith—what a coincidence. No wonder you flinched when I mentioned my friend, here." He gestured toward the mannequin. "Well, I'm about to lock up for tonight. Why don't I give your car a push to the gas station?"

David went around turning out lights and locking doors. Then he let Nancy and her friends out the front of the museum. Outside, Nancy looked up and down the empty streets. Only crickets could be heard in the quiet Salem night.

As they approached their car, George leaned over to Nancy and said, "The silver car's gone."

"Gone but not forgotten," Nancy said uneasily. Then she noticed that the driver had left a message for them—on the trunk lid of the car. *"Definitely* not forgotten!"

Everyone walked around the rented car to look at the damage. Its trunk lid was bent and scratched, as if someone had been jumping on it.

"What's this all about?" David Kaufman said. "It can't be just a missing veil."

"No, it can't," Nancy emphatically agreed.

Eventually David Kaufman's truck nosed up behind the rental car and managed to push Nancy and her two tired friends to the gas station. Then the curator waved goodbye.

In front of a small, dimly lit log cabin garage were just a couple of gas pumps. But compared to the dead quiet of the rest of Salem, the place was hopping.

Inside, the station manager was sitting with a couple of other men talking and listening to country music on a loud portable radio. Nancy tried to get his attention. But the short, stocky man ignored her, and Nancy was sure he was doing it on purpose.

Across the room Nancy noticed another driver, a tall, younger guy with platinum blond hair and an earring. He was looking up at a map taped to the wall, as if he needed directions. He glanced quickly at Nancy, then pulled a New England Patriots football cap down over his hair with a jerk and walked out.

Finally the manager got up and followed Nancy outside to the car.

"I'm usually closed at this hour. This is your lucky night," the manager said.

"Have you seen a small silver car?" Nancy

58

asked as the man stretched the hose over to the car's gas tank.

"You mean, ever in my life?" he said with a laugh.

"I mean tonight," Nancy said.

Instead of answering, he grabbed a squeegee to wash the back window. "Boy, what happened to your car?" the manager asked, looking at the trunk.

"It's been a long night," Nancy said.

"I guess so," he answered.

After the gas tank was filled, Nancy paid him, and he slowly counted the bills she handed him. "Well, now about that silver car," the man said. "I've seen three or four of 'em tonight."

"Have you known all the drivers?" Nancy asked.

"Yeah, I know 'em all. Which one you looking for?"

"Sorry," Nancy said, putting her change in her pocket. "I'm looking for the one you didn't know."

As the manager walked away, the squeal of tires cut through the night air like a siren. Nancy looked up and saw a car speeding off past the gas station. It was definitely a *silver* car!

# 7

## Brendan Thorndike's Missing Heirs

"Don't tell Bess."

It was George's voice whispering in Nancy's ear, as they watched the mysterious silver car disappear into the night. "She's fallen asleep in the backseat."

Nancy nodded.

The whole way back to Boston, Nancy and George watched silently for the silver car that was out there, somewhere, still following them.

A couple of times there was a silver car nearby, in one lane or another. But it wasn't the model they were looking for.

"It's worse when we *can't* see him," Nancy commented.

Just before they reached the hotel, Nancy motioned to George to make a quick right turn.

"I thought I just saw a car of the same make behind us," she explained. They circled the hotel three times, just to make sure they were really alone.

"The last thing we need is that guy coming after us in our hotel room!" Nancy whispered to George.

Finally, their car was parked in the hotel garage, and the girls headed up to their room. All three sprawled out on their beds.

"We need answers," George said, sipping a ginger ale from their own little room refrigerator.

"Yes," Nancy said. "But you can't get all the answers until you know all the questions."

"Okay—here's a question: Who's the guy in the silver car, and why did he follow us from the airport?" George said.

"No. The more important question is: Why didn't he *catch* us? He could have—but he always hung back," Nancy said.

Bess and George waited expectantly for Nancy to answer her own question. Nancy thought carefully for a minute to be sure she was right.

"Well, I think he didn't want to catch us. He just wanted to scare us," Nancy finally said.

"He did a great job," Bess replied. She got up from the bed and headed for the bathroom. "Tell you what. After I have a bath in that enormous tub with the gold faucets, I'll come back and help you guys solve this case. But first, I need a bubble bath!"

When Bess was gone, Nancy turned back to George. "Next question?"

"Okay—who is Markella Smith?" George asked.

"Don't know," Nancy said.

"And why did she come such a long way to steal Meredith's veil?"

"Don't know," Nancy said. "*Did* she steal Meredith's veil?"

"Don't know," George said.

Nancy rolled over and began doodling on a pad that said Ritz-Carlton on the top of every page. Although George's questions were good ones, Nancy had a bunch of even better ones herself.

Such as: Why was Meredith's ex-boyfriend, Tony, hanging around outside Cecelia's place? And why didn't Rose Strauss seem to care whether or not Nancy found the veil? And *why* was Meredith's veil so important to someone in the first place?

Nancy wrote down each question as it popped into her head.

Twenty minutes later, Bess came out of the bathroom with clean hair and a fresh attitude.

"Okay—let's get to work and figure this mystery out," she said. "Where do we start, Nancy?"

But Bess was a little too late.

"My head's spinning," Nancy said. "I think I need to cool out for a little while and forget the case. Is there anything on TV?"

Bess marched over to the television and flipped it on. Then she plopped down on her bed, wrapping up in the silk-covered comforter. Her plan of action was to sit with the remote control in one hand and a bag of sour-cream-and-chive potato chips in the other.

She flipped around the channels.

"Mrs. Clayton Bugle," a smiling, blue-eyed game-show host was saying to the contestant. "Your category is numbers. For one thousand dollars, tell me how many bristles there are in the average toothbrush."

Click! went the remote control. The screen flipped to a family sitcom. A handsome blue-eyed father was talking to his handsome blue-eyed teenage son.

"Alan, why do you always fight and argue with your sister?" the father asked.

"Gee, Dad," said the son. "Isn't it against the law to shoot her?"

The laugh track thought it was hilarious, but Bess didn't. So she changed the channel again. This time she came up with the local Boston news. The newscaster had blue eyes.

". . . no developments on the mystery all of Boston is watching—the mystery of Brendan Thorndike's missing heirs," the TV anchorman said.

"Why does everyone on television have blue eyes?" George wondered out loud.

"Shhh . . . I want to hear this," Bess said, munching a chip.

"Everyone is waiting to see if any true heirs of Brendan Thorndike will be found," the newscaster continued. A picture of a stern, elderly man appeared on the screen, captioned Brendan Thorndike. "For several weeks, the search for a son, daughter, or grandchild has been conducted by Jason Moss, the new head of the Thorndike Companies. So far, although nearly two hundred people have presented themselves claiming to be relatives of Thorndike, Jason Moss says that no legitimate heirs have turned up.

"Recently, however, Channel 8 learned that Jason Moss himself stands to inherit the entire sixty-million-dollar fortune if no other heirs are found. We talked to Mr. Moss this afternoon in his office about his role in the Thorndike empire."

Suddenly a thin and handsome man of forty came on the screen. His suit jacket was off and his shirt sleeves were rolled up. The name superimposed at the bottom of the screen said: Jason Moss, President, Thorndike Companies.

"Mr. Moss," asked the Channel 8 reporter, "as executor of Mr. Thorndike's will, it's your job to find the Thorndike children and grandchildren, isn't it?"

"Yes," Jason said with a smile. "If there are any." He seemed completely at ease in front of the cameras.

"Well, some people believe that you're deliberately trying *not* to find an heir," said the reporter. "After all, if you don't find any heirs, *you* personally will inherit the money. Isn't that true?"

"It's true that Brendan was kind enough to name me in his will," Moss said, remaining calm. "But I think you should point out to the public that I worked for Mr. Thorndike for twenty years. I know how much finding his children and grandchildren meant to him. Now that he is dead, it means that much to me."

Then the TV anchorman came back on the screen. Bess turned down the volume and looked around. Nancy and George were both completely transfixed by the story.

"Turn it back up," Nancy said quickly.

Bess pressed the remote control.

". . . following this story as it develops further. Jennifer?" the anchorman said.

He turned to the co-anchorwoman sitting next to him.

"Chuck, I think we should remind our viewers why Brendan Thorndike's heirs are being sought this way," she said.

"Sure, Jennifer. As you'll recall, Brendan Thorndike's wife, Rebecca, divorced him forty years ago, taking their children with her out of the country. She swore he would never see his children again."

"And Thorndike never did find her," Jennifer added.

"That's right," Chuck said. "At the time, they had a two-year-old daughter and a three-year-old son. They'd be about forty-two and forty-three years old now, if they're still alive."

"And what about Rebecca Thorndike?" Jennifer asked Chuck.

"She wasn't named in the will," Chuck replied. "And now for the weather we'll turn to Diane Luckey. . . ."

Nancy got up and clicked off the TV set.

"Pretty interesting," Nancy murmured to herself. Then to her friends she said, "Can you imagine that? I mean, turning your back on millions of dollars? Rebecca Thorndike must have really hated his guts."

"Yeah, well, he did look pretty repulsive," George said. "But I'll tell you who *I* don't like— Jason Moss. I don't trust him."

"Why not?" Nancy asked.

"I don't like people who smile when you call them a liar," George said. Then she turned to Bess. "What do you think, cousin? Am I right?"

"Don't call me cousin. Maybe we're not related," Bess said to George. "Maybe I was kidnapped as a baby! Maybe I was adopted and I'm really the long-lost granddaughter of Brendan Thorndike!"

Bess dissolved in laughter and fell back on the bed, hugging her pillow. "You guys had better be nice to me," she added. "I'm going to inherit *sixty million dollars!*"

Just before the sun came up the next morning, Nancy's internal alarm clock woke her up. Quietly she slipped out of bed and carried the phone, with its long cord, into the bathroom. She dialed a number.

"Hello," a young man mumbled into the phone. His voice was sleepy and angry about the early morning call.

"Tony Fiske?" Nancy asked.

"Yeah. Who is this?" he said.

"You don't know me," Nancy said. "But I promised Meredith Brody that I'd get her wedding veil back."

"Well, well," Tony said. He didn't sound surprised and he didn't sound scared. "You think I've got it?" He laughed a little.

"You're the first person *I'd* call," Nancy said. Two can play at this tough-guy game, she thought.

"Okay, let's talk about it," Tony said. "But you can't come over. We'll have to meet somewhere, and it has to be soon. How about the Boston Tea Party ship? Be there at nine o'clock. I'll be wearing—"

But Nancy didn't let him finish. "I know what you look like. I'll find you," she said.

"Hey, *miss*," Tony said. "I don't like people pushing me too hard. Just ask Meredith Brody."

The line went dead.

It was only 7 A.M., so Nancy got dressed quickly for a run. After her conversation with Tony Fiske, the early morning air felt clean and fresh. The Boston Common, across from the hotel, was perfect for running, and it looked beautiful. For a moment, though, Nancy hesitated. Maybe this wasn't the best time to go out running alone. But then she noticed that there were other early morning runners already out, so she went on.

When she got back after her run, George and Bess were still sleeping. She showered, changed, and left them a note saying she had gone to the Boston Tea Party ship to meet with Tony.

She decided to take a cab the short distance, and soon found herself boarding the popular tourist attraction. Even at nine in the morning, it was fairly crowded, mostly with kids and their parents. Nancy scanned the faces for Tony, as teenagers took snapshots of each other and a few kids tried to climb the masts.

People lined up to toss wooden tea chests overboard, just as the American rebels had done two centuries before. Nancy smiled when she realized that the chests were tied to ropes so that they could be pulled back on board for the next person in line.

By nine-thirty Tony still wasn't there, and Nancy was beginning to think he wouldn't come.

Then she heard a woman saying, "Don't push—you'll get your turn." Nancy turned around and saw Tony crowding an old man and woman. He was carrying a green tote bag and holding onto it tightly. Was the veil inside?

Nancy picked up a wooden tea chest and gave it a toss. She waited for the splash and then walked over to Tony.

"Good morning," she said. "As I mentioned on

the phone earlier, I'm looking for Meredith's stolen veil."

"Right, my heart bleeds for Meredith," Tony said. His dark looks matched his attitude. "You a friend of hers?"

"I'm the person you're going to give the veil to. Is that it?" Nancy said, pointing at the green tote bag.

"Could we talk softly? I don't want to be overheard."

"Are you afraid of something?" Nancy said.

Tony didn't answer right away. It was as though he wanted to say something but then changed his mind. "Afraid? Afraid of what?"

"Never mind," Nancy said. "I just want to ask you some questions. Like why were you waiting outside Cecelia Bancroft's house yesterday morning?"

"It's a free country, remember? Anyway, I didn't come here to be quizzed. You mentioned you wanted the veil. Are you willing to pay? 'Cause it's going to cost you. It's going to cost you a lot."

"What are you talking about?" Nancy asked.

"I figure this veil is worth ten bills to me." He enjoyed it so much he said it again. "Ten *thousand* dollars."

Nancy's mouth fell open.

"The veil isn't worth ten thousand dollars, Tony," Nancy said evenly. "It just has sentimental value to Meredith. If you have it, I wish you'd please just give it to me now."

"I don't have it," Tony interrupted. "But I could get it for you—for the right price. Ten bills. Yes or no?"

"Has someone else offered you money for the veil?" Nancy had to be sure she was hearing right. "Who?" She grabbed the green bag.

"I'm not crazy enough to tell you *that*," he said, pulling the bag away from Nancy. "Now what do you say—yes or no?"

"No. I don't have that kind of money," Nancy said. "And anyway, I wouldn't pay you for something that rightfully belongs to Meredith."

"Then just stay out of my way, and don't ruin this for me!" Tony said. "'Cause if you're not careful, you'll get hurt."

"You're threatening the wrong person," Nancy said angrily.

"I mean it," Tony said. Then he quickly left the boat, pushing people as he went.

Nancy started to chase him but she couldn't. Two strong hands had clamped down on her shoulders from behind! She craned her neck, desperately struggling to see who was trying to stop her. But it was no use. The attacker had the grip of a giant.

In an instant, the hands lifted Nancy slightly and pushed her forward over the edge of the ship—headfirst into the icy water below!

# 8

## The Boston Tea Party

Nancy hit the water hard, and sank quickly. The water was freezing. For one terrifying second she was disoriented: She lost track of which way was up. Worse yet, her clothes were becoming heavy with water, dragging her farther down.

And she was running out of air.

She tried to swim, but her leg hurt when she kicked and she went in the wrong direction. *I've got to take a breath soon,* Nancy thought. *I've got to figure out which way is up!*

Deliberately, Nancy steadied herself and looked around. Sunlight was pouring down through the water. *That's the surface,* she thought as she pointed herself in that direction and kicked again. In seconds she broke through the water and took a deep breath of air.

A lot of voices were shouting down to her from above. Bobbing in the water, Nancy could see that the ship's deck was lined with people who were watching her or taking pictures.

"Are you all right?" shouted someone who worked on the ship. He was dressed in an Indian costume, just as the American rebels had been for the Boston Tea Party.

Nancy treaded water, took another deep breath of air, and then waved. It was a small gesture, but the people above broke into a round of applause and cheers. With tired arms, she swam to the side of the dock where a crowd had formed to greet her. A Tea Party Museum employee pulled her out of the water.

Gratefully she took a beach towel from a young couple who happened to be carrying one, and dried her hair.

"Did you slip?" asked the employee from the Boston Tea Party Ship Museum.

"She didn't slip, that's for sure," said a voice in the crowd.

Nancy looked up, surprised and pleased that someone had witnessed her fall. The man who spoke up was a tall, muscular man wearing a tan, rumpled suit and a brown, wide-brimmed hat. He moved toward her through the crowd.

"What did you see?" Nancy asked, wiping strands of hair out of her face. "Did you see who pushed me?"

*Pushed?* The crowd chattered with surprise— except the man in the suit.

"Yeah, I saw plenty," he said. His voice was firm but flat and unemotional as he pulled a small spiral notebook out of his inside jacket pocket. He flipped a few pages, and started reading. "Six-feet-four male, early thirties, a hundred-eighty pounds. He had platinum blond hair, wore an earring in his left ear, and smoked thin brown cigarettes."

"Wow," said Nancy with wide eyes.

"He's not a pro, either," the man said, putting his notebook away. "He didn't beat it out of here. He stayed to watch you hit the water."

"Wait a minute," Nancy said slowly. The description had rung a bell. "Wait . . . did the guy have a cap on?"

The man got out his notebook again. "Oh, yeah, I forgot. A Patriots cap. You know him?"

Nancy shuddered. "I saw him late last night at a gas station in Salem," she said. Then she eyed the man in the brown suit. "Why were you watching him so carefully?" she asked.

"That's what I do, when I'm not enjoying the sights," the man said. He handed Nancy a business card.

It read: Harry Knox, Private Investigator.

"I could find this louse for you," Harry Knox said. "It wouldn't be any trouble. I don't like guys who push young women off national monuments."

"Thanks, Mr. Knox, but no thanks," Nancy said, returning his business card. "I don't have to find *him*. He's been following *me*. Next time, I'll be ready."

Harry Knox extended a large, meaty hand, which Nancy took and pulled herself up. "You have a lot of spirit, but not a lot of muscle," he said. He put his business card in Nancy's hand again and closed her hand into a fist. "If you need any help—I'm at the other end of the telephone."

"And then he gave me his card," Nancy said later in her hotel room. She showed Bess and George the wrinkled business card.

"Oh wow!" Bess said. She fell on her bed and laughed. "He sounds like something out of an old movie."

"He looked it, too," Nancy said. "But when he opened his notebook and started reading the description of the guy who pushed me, I didn't know whether to laugh or cry. He knew everything but the guy's dental records."

George shuddered. "You actually saw this blond guy in the gas station last night?" she said.

"He walked *this* close to me," Nancy said.

A knock on the door made her jump. Nancy laughed at herself for being nervous, but her hand fumbled with the chain on the door. Could someone have followed her back to the hotel?

"Who is it?" Nancy asked through the door.

"Room service," answered a polite voice. "I've got your lunch."

Nancy opened the door, relieved to see the familiar room service waiter. And the food smelled delicious.

Soon she and her friends were sitting around the dining table in their room, trying bites of each other's lunch and talking loudly.

"Well, while you were off swimming and having fun," George teased, "I was running up our phone bill. I've called just about every Smith in Denver. Mary, Morgan, Michelle, Margaret, Margie, and Maxine—I found them all. But I came up with zip looking for Markella."

Nancy ate the strips of cheese off her chef's salad and thought out loud. "A woman loses part of an airplane ticket in a church in Boston. It's a round-trip ticket—Denver to Boston and back to Denver," she said. "But, she never takes the flight from Denver to Boston, and she's not even scheduled on the return flight. In fact, she doesn't even *live* in Denver. Does any of this make sense?"

"Not to me," answered George. "I also called Rose Strauss in Maine and asked her about the wedding guest list. Markella Smith wasn't invited. In fact, Rose has never heard of her."

Nancy tried to sort out all of this information. But suddenly she pictured the blond guy in the Salem gas station and felt herself falling into Boston Harbor again. Her eyes glazed over.

After a silence, George slapped the table with her palm. "I think we deserve to have some fun. The case of the missing veil can wait a little longer, can't it?"

Nancy hesitated for just a moment.

"Good idea," she finally said. Then she pulled a map of Boston from her purse and blindly stuck a finger on the map. It landed on the words Freedom Trail.

"Uh-oh." Nancy laughed when she saw what she had picked. "Get ready for major league sore feet."

The Freedom Trail was a walking tour of sixteen landmarks from American revolutionary times. Even without stopping at each landmark on the tour, it took Nancy and her friends three hours to cover the territory. Nancy loved seeing all the old buildings, but her mind kept returning to the mystery of the missing veil.

"Anyone have the energy for more shopping?" Bess asked when they reached the end of the trail.

Nancy and George groaned.

But back near their hotel, the three friends window-shopped on fashionable Newbury Street until even Bess was ready to drop. Finally they went back to their room.

After showering, they dressed up for dinner and went to a wharf-side restaurant. Nancy hoped that they'd have a view of the water, and the maître d' seemed to read her mind. He led them to a big table right in the middle of a window facing the bay. But soon Bess and George were complaining that Nancy's mind had wandered again.

"It's hard to forget about the case," Nancy apologized, "even for lobster tails."

They left the restaurant at seven and went to the Beckhurst Theatre to see a new murder mystery play which had just opened there.

"I love it," Bess said. "We're really early.

People are just getting here. Now we've got time to see what everyone is wearing."

Their seats were eight rows from the stage. They were perfect seats for seeing the play, but not the best seats for people-watching. Bess and Nancy decided to stand up and turn around to watch the audience stream in.

"Blue stockings with a pink dress? Give me a break," Bess said, describing one of the theater-goers. "Ooh—now there's a gorgeous dress . . . Hey, get a look at this guy. He looks like he might be the murderer in tonight's play!"

Nancy laughed. But then suddenly she sat down and grabbed Bess's arm, pulling her into her seat, too. "Psst—Bess," Nancy whispered. "You'll never guess who just walked in."

Bess and George casually turned toward the center aisle in time to see who Nancy was talking about. There was Cecelia Bancroft.

"So?" Bess said.

"So look who she's *with!*" Nancy said softly.

All three girls studied Cecelia—the wave of her shiny blond hair, the pressure of her arm locked in that of a thin, handsome, smiling man. Cecelia's evening gown sparkled. She and the man talked to each other all the way to their third-row-center seats.

"I give up," Bess said. "Who is it?"

"It's Jason Moss," Nancy whispered, just as the curtain came up on the play. "You know—the man who controls Brendan Thorndike's sixty million dollars!"

# 9

## At the Laugh Riot

"Nancy, you're staring," George whispered in the dark. "In the wrong direction!"

The play was starting now but Nancy couldn't really concentrate on it. So many ideas were running through her head. Was Cecelia somehow involved with the missing veil? And why wasn't she out with her husband? Why was she here with Jason Moss? Did this mean the veil was somehow connected to the Thorndike affair?

BANG! A gunshot!

It came from the stage and immediately grabbed Nancy's attention. The questions in her head would have to wait—the play was getting interesting!

At intermission, the lobby of the theater was like a very large and very crowded elevator. As soon as the theater's front doors were opened, people spilled out into the street for air.

Nancy, Bess, and George squeezed through the crowded lobby, and finally found a little breathing room outside.

"I don't see Cecelia," Nancy said. "Do you?"

"There they are," George said softly. "Are you going to go up to her?"

Before Nancy could answer, Cecelia turned around and spotted all three girls.

"Aha!" she said, pulling Jason's arm. "These are the junior detectives I told you about, Jason. I can't remember their names, but I'm sure they do. And this is my husband, Jason Moss.'

Husband! Cecelia had said that she was married, but Nancy never guessed that she had kept her own last name.

"It's nice to meet you, Mr. Moss," Nancy said. "I'm Nancy Drew."

"I'll bet all of Boston would like to meet *you*," George said.

"Half of Boston already has," Jason said with a laugh. "And the other half is still lined up outside my office." He had a way of making someone feel as though he or she were the most interesting person he'd ever met.

"I thought you ladies would be on your way to Vail, Colorado," said Cecelia.

"You mean Denver," corrected Nancy. "We were *looking* for a veil. We haven't found it yet."

"Well, you'd know better than I would," Cecelia said.

"Cecelia told me about a red-haired woman and a lost airline ticket," Jason said. "It sounds very mysterious."

"Yes—it is mysterious," Nancy said. "We waited at the airport, but the woman didn't take that flight to Denver. In fact, she probably doesn't even live there."

"But we'll find her," George chimed in.

"I suspect that you are a very determined young woman," Jason said to Nancy. "You won't give up until you find what you're looking for, will you?"

"No," said Nancy.

"Good for you," Jason said. "Then I guess you and I have something in common."

Bells began ringing softly in the theater. Ushers walked through the crowd asking people to return to their seats for Act Two.

"What do you think of the play?" Cecelia asked Nancy as they re-entered the theater.

"I know who did it," Nancy said with a sly smile.

It was easy to solve mysteries in movies or the theater—but real life was different. Tony and Cecelia . . . Cecelia and Jason Moss . . . the Thorndike fortune and the veil . . . It was all too much for Nancy to consider now, especially with Act Two about to begin.

After the play was over, Cecelia and Jason walked out with Nancy, Bess, and George.

"Well—where to next?" Jason asked. "You're young. You girls should enjoy some of Boston's nightlife."

"What would you recommend?" asked Bess.

"Well, I know what I'd do if I weren't me," Cecelia said. "There's a comedy club all the young people like to go to. It's called the Laugh Riot. I'd go there."

"That's a great idea," Jason said.

Cecelia wrote down the address of the Laugh Riot comedy club and handed it to Nancy.

But when the girls were alone, they couldn't agree about what to do next.

"I need to think about the case," Nancy insisted. "It's getting very complicated."

"But tonight's our night off—remember?" George urged. "You said the veil could wait one more day."

Finally Nancy gave in and agreed that the Laugh Riot sounded great. So they hopped a cab and arrived at the Laugh Riot just in time for the late show. The small club was located on a quiet side street of Boston, but Cecelia was right about the place being popular. A line of people waiting to get in stretched around the block.

Nancy, Bess, and George got the last table, a small one by the back door. It was fun being in a popular club, but Nancy wished the room weren't quite so smoky, loud, and packed with people.

Finally a thin man wearing a black shirt and a gray tie jumped on stage and grabbed the microphone. He was the emcee. The moment the spotlight came on, people began to applaud.

"Thank you, thank you," said the young man. "Welcome to the Laugh Riot. I'm your host Richard Bellman. Thank you. Please keep clapping. It's the only way we can get the air to circulate in this dump."

The audience laughed and applauded even more and Richard went on insulting everyone for the next five minutes. Then he said, "Thank you. You're a wonderful audience, but right now I'd like to introduce our first comedian—and he's a little weird, folks,—please welcome Barry Mayonnaise."

Nancy, Bess, and George joined the applauding audience, and a very tall man wearing sweat pants and a Hawaiian shirt came on the stage. While he adjusted the microphone to reach him, a waiter came over to the girls' table.

"You girls want something to drink?" he asked.

They ordered soft drinks and the waiter said he'd be right back with them.

"Hi, everyone. My name is Barry Mayonnaise," said the comedian. "First of all, you're probably wondering how I got such an unusual name. Well, I'll be honest with you. I made it up. That's right. Barry Mayonnaise is not my real name. I changed it. My real name is Sid Mayonnaise."

The audience groaned and booed at the old joke.

"Thank you, thank you very much," said Barry. He walked back and forth across the stage, carrying the microphone and flipping the mike cord out of his way.

As Barry kept talking, the waiter worked his way through the maze of tables to bring their drinks. In between laughs they sipped them quickly because the room was hot.

"I come from another planet, where everything is exactly the opposite," Barry said. "Everyone loves to go to *slow* food restaurants on my planet. That's because you can feed your whole family there and it will only cost you a fortune. The all-time favorite sandwich is the Little Mac."

Nancy started feeling hotter and hotter.

"Something's wrong with the microphone," George whispered to Nancy. "I can't hear him too well." Her face was wet with perspiration.

Then Bess leaned over to Nancy. Her head was weaving as though her neck were made of rubber. "The whole room is going up and down, up and down," she said.

Nancy tried to reach across the table for Bess, but she couldn't move her arm. It was too heavy to lift. "George," she tried to say, but her mouth wouldn't move.

Suddenly Bess leaned forward and fell face first onto the table. *What's going on? What's happening?* Nancy thought to herself. That was the last thing Nancy saw before the whole world went black.

The next thing Nancy knew, she was cold and wet. "Why can't I move? It's so dark." It sounded like her own voice, but she felt so far away from it.

Slowly Nancy opened her eyes and tried to look around. She shivered and realized she had been talking to herself. Her heart was pounding. She wanted to move but she couldn't.

She was outside. A wet breeze blew against her damp forehead, making her even colder. Her head, legs, and arms throbbed with pain, but she suddenly realized that she couldn't even feel her hands and feet. The numbness confused Nancy until she wriggled, and discovered that her arms and legs were tied up.

Finally she became aware that she was leaning against something, something hard. She tried to turn her head to see behind her. "Bess? George?" Nancy said out loud.

There were mutters, but they sounded foggy. *Everything* seemed foggy, distant, confused.

The moon came out from behind a cloud and gleamed on a hideous face. Nancy trembled for a second until she realized that the head was only a picture carved into the top of a tombstone. She looked around. On every side of her were tall, ancient tombstones, green with age and decay. Each one had a macabre image. Skeletons dancing . . . angels with tortured faces and bird bodies . . .

"I can't move," a voice said. It was Bess. Nancy heard it clearly that time. It sounded as though Bess was about ten feet away.

Nancy lifted herself on her elbows.

"Bess, wake up." Nancy started to inch her way over to Bess. But then she stopped. Suddenly, in the moonlight, she caught a glimpse of something lying motionless at Bess's feet.

Nancy wanted to warn her friend, but it was too late. Bess was already trying to sit up. Then Bess let out a scream.

"No . . . oh, no!" Bess cried, her voice filled with panic. "Get it off me! It's a dead body—lying on my feet!"

# 10

## Graveyard Horror

Nancy bent her legs and tried to crawl across the cold, wet graveyard. The ropes cut deeply into her wrists and ankles. But it didn't matter—she had to see the dead body for herself.

In front of a massive gravestone with a cross carved through its center lay a man in ragged clothes, unmoving and unbreathing.

Bess was about to scream again when something scampered onto her legs and then off again.

"A rat!" Bess said. She tried to kick her legs but the ropes held her too tightly.

"Bess." Nancy said her friend's name softly as she scooted toward her. "Please, don't freak out now. I'll untie your ropes, if you can just lean forward a little."

"I'm cold." It was George's groggy voice. She was even farther away.

The wet ground had soaked through their clothes. It was obvious that they had been there for a while. Nancy tried not to think about the body.

"We'll warm up once we start moving," Nancy called to George. "Hold on for just a few more minutes until Bess and I can get free."

An owl hooted. Nancy heard more scampering feet. Wings flapped, twigs snapped in the darkness. The cemetery was alive with animals moving in the shadows.

"What are we doing here? And who do you think killed . . . *him?*" Bess said, tilting her head toward the body with a shiver.

"Don't talk, Bess," Nancy said. "Just hold still so I can work the ropes."

"I'm trying," Bess said.

Her fingers ached and her hands were numb from lack of circulation. But still Nancy pulled and plucked at the damp ropes that tied Bess's hands.

The moon played behind thick summer clouds, making shadows move and sway across the rows of old tombstones.

Then with a jerk and a small cry of pain Bess held her hands up into the air, free from the ropes. Nancy had done it! Then Bess quickly reached to untie Nancy's hands and legs. When Bess could move more freely, they both scampered away from the body and untied George.

They stood up and hugged each other for a moment.

"We've got to get out of here," Bess said.

"What about the dead man?" George asked.

A moonbeam fell on the corpse and Nancy

leaned closer to look at his face. Just then, the body started to move!

Bess screamed.

Then the corpse began to snore loudly.

"He's not dead," Nancy said with a small laugh. "He's just asleep."

"Phew!" Bess said. "Let's see if we can find our bags and then get out of here before he wakes up!"

Looking around, the girls realized that the cemetery was actually quite small—and it was located in the heart of downtown Boston. They found their purses lying near a tombstone, and then they quickly walked through the cemetery's creaky iron gates. In no time they were outside on the sidewalk again.

For a while they walked without saying anything. Then at the first telephone booth they found, Nancy called the police. She was surprised but glad when Lieutenant Flood answered the phone. He was on night duty for another officer.

"We were at the Laugh Riot," Nancy told him, "when all of a sudden we blacked out. Someone must have put knockout drops in our sodas."

Flood promised Nancy he'd have a squad car pick them up in five minutes. He'd also send an officer to the Laugh Riot in the morning to get to the bottom of what had happened.

"I thought you were just after a car license, Nancy," the policeman said. "I wish I'd known you were going to get involved in something this dangerous. What's it all about?"

"I'll tell you after I eliminate one more suspect," Nancy said.

Nancy hung up the phone. Bess was yawning and George had dark circles under her eyes from being so tired. "I hope the police get here soon," Nancy said.

Moments later two officers arrived and took a report from the girls. Then the policemen took them back to the Ritz in the squad car. Inside their room, they found that the hotel maid had turned down the bed sheets and left them each a wrapped chocolate mint on their pillows.

*She comes in and does all this and we never see her,* Nancy thought to herself as she stretched her tired and bruised body out on the bed. *There's someone else out there we never see. And all he wants to do is hurt us.*

Nancy turned out her lamp, then lay awake thinking about the case. She couldn't stop wondering about Cecelia Bancroft and her role in all that had happened that night. She was the one who'd steered them to the comedy club. Had she set them up to be drugged? And could Cecelia somehow be involved in the disappearance of the veil? If so, Nancy thought, was the veil linked to Jason Moss and the Thorndike heirs? One last question nagged at Nancy before she drifted off to sleep: How was Tony Fiske involved with Cecelia?

* * *

Nancy set out early the next morning to follow up an important hunch. Her hunch was that Tony Fiske could tell her whether Cecelia was as innocent as she seemed. Not wanting to wake her friends, Nancy ducked into the bathroom to use the phone. She dialed Tony's number.

"Hello," a woman's voice said. "I'm sorry, but the number you have reached has been disconnected. If you wish an operator to—"

Nancy hung up. But the fact that Tony's phone had been disconnected didn't prove anything, she decided. Maybe he hadn't paid his bill.

Quickly she got dressed, scribbled a note to Bess and George, and drove to Tony's apartment.

It was a small apartment in an old building. His door was at the end of three flights of stairs. Nancy listened at the door before knocking. A radio blasted out a symphony.

That's strange music for Tony, Nancy thought as she knocked on the door and waited.

At last the radio was snapped off and the door opened. To Nancy's surprise, a pleasant-looking woman stood facing her. The woman's face was paint-splattered, and she had white paint in her black curly hair, too.

"Is Tony Fiske here?" Nancy asked.

The woman laughed and opened the door wide. The apartment was empty except for a ladder, cans of paint, and brushes.

"He's gone," the woman said. "*Gone.* And I *love* it. He paid me the back rent he owed—five full months. And he told me to get rid of all his stuff, because he's leaving town for good. Hope he didn't owe you any money."

"Did he have a lot?" Nancy asked.

"For Tony, two coins to rub together is a lot," the woman said. "But, yes, for once he had a lot."

"Did he say where he was going?" Nancy asked, but she didn't really expect an answer.

"As a matter of fact, he did. He said he'd never been to Bermuda, and it must be great this time of year."

Bermuda! That's where Meredith and Mark were spending their honeymoon!

"I've got to call Meredith and warn her," Nancy said, thinking out loud.

"Who's Meredith?" the landlady asked.

Nancy snapped back to the present.

"Oh, a friend. Thank you—you've been a lot of help," Nancy said and left quickly. She drove back to the hotel, but got a bit delayed in the tangle of Boston traffic.

Dashing into the hotel room, Nancy called hello to Bess and George and went straight to the phone.

"Do we have Meredith's number in Bermuda?" she asked George, picking up the receiver.

But Bess and George didn't answer. They had exciting news of their own.

"Nancy," Bess said, "something arrived—"

Nancy put the phone back on the hook—and immediately it rang. She picked it up again. It was Police Lieutenant Flood.

"Morning, Nancy," he said in his raspy voice.

91

"You want to hear what happened to you at the Laugh Riot last night?"

"Yes," said Nancy.

Suddenly she noticed what George and Bess were so excited about. There was a large box wrapped in brown paper sitting on her bed.

"The waiter remembers you and your friends real well," Lieutenant Flood said. "He says he was getting your drinks ready when a guy at the bar stopped him. The guy said that *he'd* like to pay for your drinks. He told the waiter he was a friend. Later, when you three started feeling the knockout drugs, this guy told the waiter he'd take care of you. He helped you, one by one, through the kitchen, out the back door, and into his car. That's all anyone at the club saw. You want to hear his description, kid?"

Nancy answered for the lieutenant. "Six-feet-four, one-hundred-and-eighty-pound male with bleached blond hair, earring in the right ear, and wearing a Patriots cap."

"I don't believe it. Who told you that?"

"Harry Knox," Nancy said.

"Harry Knox? He's a dinosaur," Lieutenant Flood laughed. "He'd make a good cop except he hates to play by the rules. So how'd he know about this guy at the club?"

"He didn't," Nancy said. "I just made a good guess. Harry saw that same guy push me off the Tea Party ship yesterday."

"Kid, how'd you like me to have a man cover you? This sounds too dangerous."

Nancy thought about the offer for a minute. It was tempting, but . . .

"Please, don't, Lieutenant Flood," Nancy finally said. "I don't think I'll be able to catch this guy if you do. I've got to go now."

"You know there's an old saying about giving someone enough rope and they'll hang themselves, kid."

"I know, Lieutenant, but I'm hoping I can tightrope-walk on it instead," Nancy said.

"Give my regards to your father," the policeman said before he hung up.

As soon as Nancy was off the phone, she and Bess and George all started talking at once.

"What's in that box?" Nancy asked, pointing to the package on the bed.

"It came for you while you were gone," George said.

"Special delivery by a messenger," Bess said.

"Let's open it."

The label said: TO Nancy Drew, C/O The Ritz-Carlton Hotel.

Nancy noticed that there was no return address on the package. She tore away the brown parcel paper. Inside was a large white cardboard box. Nancy lifted the box. It was lightweight. Then she set it down and began to lift the lid. All three girls pressed their faces close to see what was inside.

"I don't believe it," Bess said. "It's Meredith's veil!"

# 11

## A Veil of Mystery

Nancy took the long, lace veil out of the white box. For the moment, it didn't matter where it had come from or who had sent it. She was just happy to hold it in her hands and let it billow to the carpeted floor. And George and Bess were so happy they jumped up and began dancing around the hotel room.

Nancy spread the veil across the bed, running her fingers over it, tracing the intricate patterns in the beautiful handmade lace.

"I can't believe it. Someone sent you the veil," Bess said.

"Someone who thought you were getting too close to the truth," George said. "I can't wait to call Meredith and tell her!"

But Nancy's face had become more serious.

"Yes—we do have to call Meredith. But I'm afraid we have only bad news."

That stopped George and Bess cold.

"What are you talking about?" asked Bess.

"George, do you still have Meredith's engagement picture?" Nancy asked.

George fished through her purse for a newspaper clipping Meredith had sent her. She found it in her address book and diary.

The three girls looked carefully at the newspaper photo of Meredith. Beaming face, glowing smile—all set off by the white wedding dress and veil she wore. Only the front of the veil showed in the picture.

"See—it's just as I remembered," Nancy said. "A feathered border." She ran her finger up and down along the veil in the photo, touching the pattern of fine feathers along the border of Meredith's veil. Then she picked up the edge of the veil on her bed and ran her finger along the edge.

"Scalloped border," Bess said. Her heart sank.

"You mean, it's not Meredith's veil?" George said.

"It's not Meredith's veil," Nancy repeated, shaking her head. "I wanted it to be so badly that for a minute I thought it was."

Just to make certain, they called Meredith and Mark in Bermuda. The newlyweds were having a great time, Meredith said, explaining why she hadn't been in touch.

"I know I said I'd call every day," Meredith went on happily. "But now that we're married and out of Boston, I feel so much better. It seems kind of silly to have worried about an astrologer's prediction. What could go wrong? The world is such a wonderful place!"

Nancy hated to burst the bubble for Meredith, but she had to warn her about Tony.

"There's something I have to tell you," Nancy began. "I think Tony Fiske may have gone to Bermuda looking for you."

Hearing that, Meredith's voice became tense.

"Why won't he leave me alone?" Meredith said. It was more a plea than a question.

Then Nancy told Meredith about the veil that had been delivered anonymously to the hotel. When she described it, Meredith confirmed that it was *not* hers.

"Listen, I hope you're not going to any trouble," Meredith said. "I mean, I'd love to have my veil back, but it *is* only a veil, after all. You and Bess and George aren't in any danger, are you?"

Nancy hesitated before answering. "We're always very careful," she said diplomatically.

Later that morning, the three girls lay on the grass in the Boston Common, letting the sun bake away their bruises and aches.

"Well, what now?" George asked.

"I never want to see another comedian. I know that," Bess said, thinking of the Laugh Riot. "In fact, I'd appreciate it if you two wouldn't make any jokes until we get home."

But Nancy wasn't thinking about the Laugh Riot at all. She was sorting through her mental file of details from three days ago, when Meredith's veil was stolen.

"Tony Fiske is out of the country," Nancy said.

"And we may never find out how he fits into this. So we're going to have to go in a different direction."

George and Bess waited until Nancy had made her decision.

"I don't know who the blond-haired man is. But I keep coming back to Cecelia Bancroft," Nancy went on. "There still could be some connection between Cecelia and the veil."

"Because she was across the street when it was stolen?" George asked.

Nancy nodded, then added, "And because she steered us to the Laugh Riot, where our drinks were tampered with."

Bess sat up and lifted her large round sunglasses onto her forehead. "Well, I'm more interested in Cecelia's connection to Jason Moss."

Nancy smiled. "Me, too," she said. "Cecelia and Jason might inherit the entire Thorndike fortune very soon. I don't know if that has anything to do with anything, but maybe our case is somehow connected to the Thorndikes."

Suddenly Nancy jumped up with a look of satisfaction on her face.

"We're going to Cape Cod!" she announced, pulling Bess and George up off the ground.

Cape Cod, Nancy knew, was not only a beautiful seaside resort area. It was also the location of the Thorndike mansion. Perhaps there she could find a clue to help her connect the Thorndike case to the missing veil.

After packing sweaters and picking up a small

lunch from a nearby carry-out store, the girls piled into the rental car and drove out of town quickly.

When they finally pulled up to the Thorndike house two hours later, a surge of excitement rippled through Nancy. The beautiful mansion, which sat on a steep bluff overlooking the ocean, drew her like a magnet.

But there was also another quality to the house —a sinister quality—which didn't escape Nancy's notice. The massive dark stone walls of the three-story building seemed to boast of a strength that would stand up to anything, even the power of the sea.

By the time Nancy and her friends parked the car it was 4 P.M. They were just in time to take the day's final tour of the mansion. Already, more than twenty people were holding tickets. ·

"Hi, everybody. My name is Robert, and welcome to Thorn Hill," their tour guide said in a friendly voice. He smiled a lot when he talked and made eye contact with everyone. "Before we move into the mansion, there are a couple of rules we'd like you to know about," he said. "You can't take pictures. In fact, we don't want you to take *anything*. And please watch children carefully. If anything gets broken, it's my neck."

The group chuckled and the tour began in the entryway of the house. Robert obviously loved every inch and corner of the mansion. He talked for a long time about every architectural detail— the plaster, the arches, the molding, the leaded

98

glass, the marble floors, and so on. Nancy soaked this information in, but she was looking for something—she wasn't quite sure how to put it. A less public detail.

On the second floor, the group entered a library. In addition to the hundreds of leather-bound books, the library held dozens of photos of Brendan Thorndike posing with famous people.

"Where are the Thorndike family portraits?" Nancy asked, gazing around the room.

Robert smiled in reply, as if to say that he, too, would like to know Mr. Thorndike better. "Mr. Thorndike removed all of his personal possessions five years ago when he moved out of the mansion," Robert said.

Nancy's heart sank, but still she combed each room for something—a clue, a tiny shred of information that could connect Cecelia to the missing veil. Everywhere she looked, however, her eyes found only one thing: the Thorndike family crest.

Brendan Thorndike had marked all of his possessions with it. It was on the furniture, on wall hangings and quilts, even on the spines of every leather-bound book in the library.

It was a fascinating, complex pattern of blooming tulips, arranged in a circle or wreath. The flowers' stems were twisted thickly, tightly together into an abstract configuration in the circle's center. Nancy couldn't decide whether the twisted stems looked more like a web or a net.

"Nice place to visit," George said to Nancy, "but I wouldn't want to live here."

"It *is* pretty gloomy," Nancy agreed.

"Be careful. This place may be mine someday, when I'm declared the missing heir!" Bess said with a grin.

Then Robert brought them to what he called the loneliest room of the house. It was Thorndike's private study.

"This is the room where Mr. Thorndike kept his records of his attempts to find his children and wife," Robert explained. "He used to keep all their photos in this room as well. But when he moved out, he ordered that every photo of his wife, his son, and his daughter be removed from the house."

"It's so sad. Why did his wife leave?" Bess asked the tour guide.

"Mr. Thorndike never said," Robert answered. "All I know is that after five years of marriage and two children, Mrs. Rebecca Thorndike just left. It broke his heart."

"Not at first," Nancy interrupted. "Only when he was an old man."

For a moment, Robert and Nancy stared at each other. She could see that he didn't like anyone making a negative comment about Thorndike.

"Why do you say that?" Robert asked.

"You can see it in the photos of Thorndike," Nancy said. "His eyes are as cold as steel, even after his wife took their children away. His work

100

is what counted to him." Nancy pointed to a photo of Thorndike as an old man sitting in his library. "In his later years, his eyes grew softer," Nancy said. "Maybe he finally realized how much he missed them."

"You're very observant," said a woman in a flowered hat, looking over Nancy's shoulder at the photo.

"Well, there's a lot more to see, folks," Robert said, changing the subject quickly. "Let's go into the master bedroom."

The bedroom was large, with closets full of clothes. The chests of drawers were of dark, hand-carved mahogany. On every drawer was a Thorndike crest painted in gold leaf.

Then it was on to the dining room.

"The table is set," said Robert, "with the oldest china in the house. It belonged to Mr. Thorndike's British ancestors and was given to the young Mrs. Thorndike as a wedding present."

Everyone on the tour, including Nancy, Bess, and George, leaned over the table to get a good look at the china. Its pattern was, as they expected, the Thorndike crest.

"There's something odd about this china," Nancy said.

"I don't see it," George said. "Give me a hint."

"The crest is different," Nancy said. "But I don't know how. I'm going to check it out." She moved toward the dining-room door.

"Excuse me," said Robert. "Where are you going?"

101

"Could I go back to the master bedroom?" Nancy asked.

"If you lost something, one of the guards will find it," Robert said.

"I didn't lose anything," Nancy said pleasantly. "I'd like to look at something again."

Robert shook his head. "Sorry," he said. "This is the last tour and you're not allowed to return to any of the rooms unescorted."

"It'll only take a minute," Nancy said.

"It'll take less than that for me to get fired," Robert said.

"You can come again tomorrow, dear," said the woman in the flowered hat. "Then you can see everything."

Exasperated, Nancy stepped back into her place among the other tour guests. But outside, when the tour was over, she saw a chance and took it. While everyone else was invited to wander through the tulip garden, Nancy quietly slipped back into the house.

Nancy felt like a criminal as she sneaked upstairs into the master bedroom to look at the gold-leaf crest hand-painted on the drawers of the mahogany chest. Then she hurried into the dining room to look at the old china plates.

"There's a difference, all right," Nancy whispered, looking carefully.

The older version of the crest, on the china, was less complicated. The ring of tulips was the same, but at the center, where the stems met, it was much less thickly tangled.

Quickly Nancy took out a pencil and fished out the largest piece of scrap paper she could find in her purse. Then she leaned against the dining-room wall, sketching the china version of the crest. Was that a footstep in the hall? Was someone coming? With her heart pounding, she hurried back into the bedroom and sketched the crest on the mahogany drawers.

Back outside in the garden, Bess and George hadn't missed her at all. Nancy waited until the other visitors had driven away. Then, standing in the parking lot, she showed her friends the two drawings.

"What do you think?" Nancy asked Bess.

Bess sat on the hood of their car and looked closely at the paper. "Maybe the crest changed because the artists changed over the years," she said. "The china is very old, you know."

Bess handed the paper to George who stared at it for a while. George shook her head.

"Sure, the crests are different," George said. "But so what? I don't see any hidden words or secret messages."

Just then, George turned the paper over in her hands. On the other side, there was the address of the Laugh Riot. Suddenly she sat up very tall. "Guys, I don't know about the crest. But I do know one thing. I've seen this handwriting before. It's totally familiar."

"Sure," Nancy said. "It's Cecelia's. That's the paper she used when she wrote down the address of the comedy club."

George shook her head. "No. I mean I've seen it *somewhere else.*"

Nancy studied the paper for a minute. Then she started digging in her purse with a wild kind of excitement. "George, you're right, you're brilliant, and you're wonderful!" she shouted.

"I know," said George. "But what are you talking about?"

Nancy pulled her wallet from her purse and found in it the airline ticket made out to Markella Smith. She handed the ticket to Bess and George.

"The handwriting is exactly the same!" they cried out together.

The handwriting *was* exactly the same, Nancy knew now. Which meant that Cecelia had written Markella Smith's airline ticket. Which meant that Markella Smith probably didn't exist.

"Wait a minute . . ." Bess said, trying to piece the story together. "You mean to tell me Markella was Cecelia Bancroft all along?"

Nancy nodded her head as she quickly got into the car.

# 12

## Cecelia's Party

"I knew I had seen that handwriting somewhere," George said as they started the two-hour drive from the Cape back to Boston. "I must have looked at that airline ticket a hundred times—while I was calling every Smith in Denver."

"Yes," Nancy said. "Cecelia probably took this phony ticket to the church the day she met us there, and dropped it in the church stairway when George wasn't looking."

"But why?" George said.

"I think it was a trick to get us to go to Denver and get out of town," Nancy said. "And now I'm sure that Cecelia had something to do with stealing Meredith's veil. Cecelia might even be the red-haired woman who tricked Meredith!"

"Wouldn't that be weird?" Bess said. "I mean, if Meredith were here, she could identify her in a minute! But she's in Bermuda, and we never saw the red-haired woman. Meanwhile we're running all over Boston with Cecelia as though she's our best friend."

"She's a very cagey woman," Nancy said. "But I knew she'd make a mistake sometime—and I hoped I'd be there to catch her."

"What now? Call the police?" George asked.

"Not quite yet," Nancy said. "We don't really have enough proof. An airline ticket with her handwriting on it doesn't prove she stole the veil. I think we should pay Cecelia a visit."

By the time they reached Boston it was almost eight, and all three girls were starving. But a rushed dinner was all Nancy would allow her friends. She was eager to get to Cecelia's.

After dinner the three of them jumped back into the rental car and Nancy outlined her plan.

"The two of you will keep Cecelia talking, while I try to slip away and search the house for the veil."

But when George pulled the car up in front of 1523 Chestnut Street, the plan hit a snag.

Cecelia and Jason's house was aglow with bright lights and music. Even from the street, Nancy could see people moving in every room. New guests arrived as quickly as their limos could pull up in front of the walk. There was a party going on—that was clear.

"Uh-oh," said Bess to Nancy. "We're going to need an invitation to talk to Cecelia tonight."

"Maybe this isn't the best time to try," George added. "Cecelia will be too distracted to talk to us."

"I know," Nancy answered with a sly grin.

"That means it's a perfect time to search her house for Meredith's veil."

Nancy left George and Bess out front, and went around to the back of the house. There wasn't really a yard, but candles and lanterns had made the courtyard festive with twinkling lights. There were tables of food and drink, and benches where the guests could sit and talk. And while a guitarist played classical music, people walked here and there, mingling and chatting to each other. With so many guests, it was going to be easy for Nancy to blend in. Getting into the house and keeping out of Cecelia's way was a more difficult problem.

Well, if I'm supposed to look like a guest, Nancy thought, I've got to act like one.

So as she made her way across the courtyard, she stopped to put cheeses, crackers, fresh vegetables, a slice of lemon cake, and a cup of punch on a plate.

It was working and it was going to work—unless someone asked her who she was.

"Hello, who are you?" called a man with a kind face and a spicy chicken wing in his hand.

"I'm Nancy," she said, suddenly taking a serious interest in her watch. "Who are you?"

"I'm Harold," said the man. "Are you timing me?"

"No," said Nancy.

"Are you with someone?" Harold asked.

"I came with two friends," said Nancy.

107

She tried to walk away after each answer, but Harold followed. As he spoke he plucked hors d'oeuvres off trays carried by the catering helpers.

"Tell me, Nancy, are you a lover of art, or are you like me? I'm here because when Jason Moss tells you to come see his newest acquisition, you come."

"Actually, I know Cecelia better than I know Jason," Nancy said. "Would you excuse me? I promised to meet her right away."

Nancy handed Harold her plate and moved quickly, zigzagging through the crowd. The best route was probably to sneak in through the back door of the house. But just as Nancy approached the back steps, Cecelia came out that door. Nancy held her breath and stood statue-still.

"Hello, hello, everybody," Cecelia said. "We're going to unveil the painting now. So everyone come inside to look and don't just feed your silly faces."

Then she disappeared. Nancy let out her breath with relief. Had Cecelia noticed her? Nancy knew Cecelia well enough to be sure of one thing: Cecelia could have spotted Nancy and not even flinched.

Casually Nancy moved into the house with everyone else. But as the crowd flowed into the living room, Nancy took a detour and followed the first stairway up.

Pausing on the first landing, she noticed a hall lined with several doors. Quietly she looked in

one bedroom and then the next, listening carefully for footsteps behind her. Which room was
Cecelia's?

When she found it, Cecelia's bedroom was
unmistakable. It was painted bright pink.

With the door closed behind her, Nancy
started looking through closets and bureau drawers. Where would Cecelia hide the veil? It wasn't
in any of the more obvious places, so Nancy
moved quickly to Cecelia's dressing table and
studied it carefully.

At first, the table looked messy, but Nancy
soon realized that it was really very orderly, with
straight rows of perfume bottles, hair clips,
brushes, and puffs. Kind of like Cecelia's mind,
Nancy thought. Her conversations *sounded*
chaotic—but underneath, she really knew exactly what she was doing.

Then suddenly Nancy sat very still, and her
heart started to race with excitement. Right in
front of her, leaning against the large round
mirror, there were two photographs. One was of
Cecelia's dog Licorice wearing a graduate's cap
and tassel. The other was of a smiling young man.
He was tall and muscular, with dark hair that was
long and wavy. And his face was shadowed because of the Patriots cap he was wearing.

Nancy grabbed the photo off the table with
both hands and stared at it. The hair was a
different color. He wasn't wearing an earring.
But there was no mistaking it: The face was that
of the blond man in the silver car!

Faster and faster her pulse pounded. This was what she was looking for! But then something, a sound, made Nancy turn her head toward the door. Something outside was making little scratching noises. The little scratching became loud scratching and then loud barking. Licorice had found her!

Nancy was frozen, paralyzed, with the photo in her hands as the doorknob turned and the door to Cecelia's bedroom began to open.

# 13

## Family Secrets

As soon as the door was open wide enough, Licorice leaped in like a miniature guard dog. He bounced and barked at Nancy. But Nancy was not watching the dog. Her eyes were fixed on the door, waiting to see who was standing in the hall. The pulse in Nancy's throat pounded so hard she couldn't swallow. The door kept opening slowly. When it opened wide enough for a person to fit through, a woman walked in.

She and Nancy stared at each other. It wasn't Cecelia.

"Oh! There *is* someone in here," the woman said. Her many bangles clinked, and her long silk dress rustled as she circled Nancy. "I thought Licorice was just being crazy. Of course, I really think a lot less of him than that. He never barks at me. He only bites. I keep hoping he'll chase a ball in front of a steamroller someday."

Nancy told herself to smile and try to look relaxed. On the inside she was waiting for the woman to ask why she was in Cecelia's bedroom.

The woman crossed the room to Cecelia's dressing table. She looked in the vanity mirror and brushed her short brown hair.

"My name's Greta," the woman said.

"Nancy."

With Greta's back turned and Licorice quiet for the moment, Nancy began moving slowly toward the door.

"So what are you doing up here?" Greta asked.

Nancy froze. "Well . . ." she said hesitantly.

"Are you hiding out so you don't have to look at the dreadful thing they call a painting? I know I am," Greta said.

"Yes, sort of," said Nancy.

Greta helped herself to a spray from one of Cecelia's perfume bottles. She didn't seem to be wondering why Nancy was there at all. In fact, she appeared happy for the company.

"Have you known the Mosses long?" Greta asked in a friendly voice.

"Just a few days, but I'm getting to know them better all the time," Nancy said. Her eyes drifted to the doorway. She knew that at any moment someone else could walk into the room—and that someone else could be Cecelia.

"I've known Cecelia for years," said Greta. "We're best friends. I love her, faults and all."

"What faults does she have?" Nancy asked.

Greta sat down on the bed, and Licorice, who had gotten there first, started growling. "When we were kids," Greta said, "our motto was You can never be too thin or too rich. Well, in time, Cecelia decided to cut that motto in half. Money. That's all she cares about now—and this disgusting dog."

Greta took the photo of the guy with the Patriots cap from Nancy.

"Do you know who that is?" Nancy asked.

"It's hard to believe that's Frazier, isn't it?" said Greta. "He's changed a lot too. He's got all that blond hair now, and he even wears a diamond earring sometimes. But I can remember when he was just Cecelia's tagalong little brother."

Cecelia's brother! So that's who the guy with the platinum hair was! Frazier Bancroft had done just about everything he could to frighten and hurt Nancy and her friends. Nancy had to sit down quickly, but she tried not to let Greta see that this information was a shock.

Nancy wanted to leave. She had to get out of there fast. But Greta wanted to talk.

"I remember once when we were freshmen in high school. . . ." Greta said.

It sounded like the beginning of a long story. So while Greta was drifting into it, Nancy made a quick, furtive move toward Licorice with her hand. The dog did just what Nancy hoped he would do. He snapped at her hand with a bark, leaving two long red welts on her skin.

The bite was minor, but Nancy made a major production out of it. "Ouch," she cried, holding her hand, cradling it with the other.

"Join the club, dear," Greta said. "Is it very bad?"

"I don't know," Nancy said. "I think I'd better wash it."

Nancy took off for the bedroom door and didn't look back as she went downstairs and steered herself straight for the front door and out.

Bess and George were sitting in the car parked across the street. When Nancy appeared, George started up the engine.

"Listen to this," Nancy said, climbing into the car. "I didn't find the veil, but I found out who the guy with the blond hair is. He's Cecelia's brother, Frazier Bancroft."

It took a little while for that to sink in.

Bess and George had a million questions, and Nancy wanted to unwind. So when they drove past the blinking sign of a late-night coffee shop they decided to stop.

"Tell us everything," Bess said as the three of them sat down at a booth.

After they had ordered onion rings and sodas, Nancy told her friends about sneaking upstairs and then meeting Greta.

"Greta is Cecelia's best friend, so she must know what she's talking about," Nancy said.

George, who was sitting near the window, twirled an onion ring on her finger. "You know," she said, "if Cecelia doesn't have the veil, now we've got a pretty good idea who does. Her brother."

"I'm *sure* he does," Bess said.

"Okay," George continued. "Then why don't we just find out where he lives and get the veil?"

"Not tonight," Nancy said firmly. "It's too late and Frazier's probably asleep. We've got to go when he's not home."

"But maybe he's out at Cecelia's party right now. We won't know unless we call him. That's my department. So let me out," Bess said to Nancy.

"Wait a minute, Bess," Nancy said. "If he answers and you just hang up, he might get suspicious. Calling him has to be done carefully."

"Don't worry. I'm good at this. Now let me out."

Nancy let her out, but she and George followed Bess to the pay phone in the back of the quiet restaurant.

Bess got Frazier's number from information and then everyone squeezed around the telephone earpiece to hear if he picked up.

"Hello," a man's voice said.

"Hi, Max. It's Betsy. How're you doing?" Bess said.

"Who's this?"

"It's me, Betsy. Remember me, Max?"

"This isn't Max."

"Is Max there?"

"You've got the wrong number or something."

"No way," Bess said. "Who's this?"

"This is Frazier and I don't know you from a hole in the ground. So will you let me get some sleep? I've got work to do in the morning."

"Sorry," Bess said and hung up.

"You're wonderful, Bess," said Nancy. "Now we even know *when* to go there—tomorrow morning when he leaves for work."

As they paid their bill, the guy at the cash register grumbled, "Don't you girls have anything better to do than make funny phone calls?"

"We lead very boring lives," Bess said. "It's the only excitement we get."

Frazier Bancroft lived in a small blue house in a neighborhood of mostly red brick houses. Apparently, Nancy thought to herself, liking bright colors was one of the Bancroft family traits— along with stealing wedding veils and chasing and kidnapping teenage detectives.

Still, as Nancy, Bess, and George waited in their rental car outside Frazier's house the next morning, she couldn't help wondering what he was really like. With his earring and wild blond hair, he just didn't look like the typical creep. In fact, if he didn't have those two deep creases around his mouth, Nancy would have thought he was almost good-looking.

At six-thirty he finally came out of his house in blue jeans, a work shirt, and his Patriots cap. Nancy, Bess, and George waited until he drove away in his silver car. Then they crept around to the back of his house.

116

Thanks to Frazier, the house wasn't too hard to get into. He hadn't locked his windows and there was no security system. George climbed in through a kitchen window and soon all three girls were inside.

But right away Nancy realized that finding the veil wasn't going to be so easy.

Frazier Bancroft's apartment was perfectly neat, with everything put away in what seemed like a million closets and built-in cabinets and chests.

"The veil could be anywhere," George said.

"Maybe he has a filing system—you know, like a library," said Bess.

The telephone rang loudly. The girls started, but the answering machine clicked on after the second ring.

"Hi, this is Frazier. I just stepped out. I'll call you back in ten minutes. . . . BEEEP!"

The girls looked at each other nervously.

"Fraz, dear, this is Cecelia. Call me ASAP. Toodles," said a familiar voice from the answering machine.

One thing was now clear in Nancy's mind. If the veil was there, she was going to have to find it fast.

While Bess and George searched upstairs, Nancy attacked the living room. She opened one drawer after another, one cabinet after another. Magazines, stationery, bills, check receipts . . . This guy was organized. There was a whole drawer of seashells and another whole drawer filled with different kinds of knives. Too bad he didn't have a drawer for veils.

Then Nancy heard a loud crash upstairs. She sucked in her breath. Had they broken something?

"Don't worry," Bess shouted a second later. "Nothing's broken."

Nancy was working in the dining room by then. Silverware, plates, tablecloths, napkins, candlesticks, candles, matches—everything had its own drawer.

"Five minutes are up!" yelled George.

Slam-bang. Drawers opening and closing. The linen closet—towels, washcloths, soap—and a large plastic trash bag with a lace wedding veil! Nancy pulled it out and examined it closely. The veil had a feathered border—just like the one in Meredith's photo!

"Hold everything!" Nancy yelled. "I've got it. I'm holding it! I've actually got Meredith's veil!"

Bess and George dashed down the stairs and joined Nancy in the dining room to look at the veil.

"Great," George said. "Now let's get out of here."

The girls slipped out the back door and got into their car.

As Bess drove away, she said, "I can't believe it. We've really got it this time. Meredith's own veil."

"I wonder what Frazier will be more angry

about. Our finding the veil or messing up his house," George said.

Nancy rode in silence for the next few miles, enjoying her success. Why didn't it feel like a perfect triumph? Something was still nagging at her in the back of her mind.

"Every time I think I've solved this case, something tells me I haven't," Nancy said. She spread the veil out in her lap and admired the delicate rose pattern. It was a beautiful, simple design—just one enormous rose with many petals clustered in the middle.

"You found the thieves and you found the veil," George said. "Sounds to me like the score is two-nothing in your favor."

"Cecelia wouldn't steal something for the fun of it. She'd only steal this veil if it were worth a fortune," Nancy said. She thought for a moment, and then suddenly the answer seemed so clear. Cecelia and money. Of course! "What's the only big money up for grabs these days?" Nancy said.

"The Thorndike fortune," Bess answered quickly.

"Right. And I think I see the connection," Nancy said.

She looked up and saw that they were stopped at a red light. Across the street was a small cluster of shops. Impulsively, Nancy hopped out of the car with the veil. "I'll be right back," she shouted.

"What should we do?" Bess called. "Park the car?"

"Yes," Nancy said. "Wait for me!"

Nancy zipped across the street and into a photocopy shop.

"Hi. I want you to blow something up," she said to the clerk.

"This is a copy shop, not a terrorist headquarters," said the young man behind the counter. Then he laughed with his entire thin body. "I never get tired of that joke," he said. "Anyway, this is a do-it-yourself place. Pick a machine. I'm just here to bother people."

Nancy put her two sketches of the Thorndike crest on the glass and enlarged them 155%. But the enlargements still weren't as big as she wanted so she enlarged the copies. The crests looked bigger, but still not perfect.

"What are these?" the shop clerk asked, examining the crests.

"They're sketches of family crests," Nancy explained. "I'm trying to enlarge the sketched designs to match this." Nancy took the veil out of its bag and looked at the rose tatted on the center back. Then she made a third set of copies. This time the enlargements were as big as the rose on the veil.

The clerk pointed to the sketch from the mahogany drawers. "This one's all junked up and busy in the middle. And this one," he said about the crest from the old plates, "is simpler. It's less crowded in the center."

"That's right," Nancy said. "Watch this."

She placed the veil over the photocopy of the

crest from the china plates. The rose fit perfectly in the uncluttered center of the design.

"Hey, now that one looks just like the other drawing," the clerk said.

"I know," Nancy said, smiling triumphantly and thinking to herself: *That's because* this rose *is part of the famous Thorndike crest!*

# 14

## Kidnapped!

Nancy quickly paid the clerk for the copies and then carefully laid the veil back in its plastic bag.

She rushed out of the store, almost bumping into someone on the sidewalk.

"Sorry," Nancy said, looking up and down the street for the rental car and Bess and George.

BRAAP!—a car horn blast.

Bess was signaling to Nancy from across the street and halfway down the block. But Nancy's mind was spinning with all the new information. She saw the passing cars and her friends waving. But she didn't see the silver car parked right across from the store, nor did she see the tall blond man coming right up behind her.

Nancy started to cross the street, weaving through the traffic until she reached the yellow line in the middle. I have a lot of questions for Meredith's grandmother, Nancy thought to herself, such as question number one: Where did she get a veil with the Thorndike crest on it?

Suddenly hands grabbed her from behind, locking her arms tightly.

"Nancy!" Bess's voice came from down the street.

Nancy turned her head and looked straight into the glaring face of Frazier Bancroft. The sun glinted off his diamond earring.

"Let me help you across the street," he said, forcing her quickly, roughly toward his car. "Don't you know you can get hurt jaywalking?"

Nancy struggled to get away, but Frazier was too strong. He flung open the door on the driver's side of his car and brutally shoved Nancy inside, pushing her across the front seat.

Nancy could see George and Bess running toward the silver car as Frazier slipped behind the wheel. But before they reached the car, Frazier slammed and locked the car doors tight.

Nancy's last chance to tell her friends about the veil was slipping away.

"The veil!" she mouthed to them through the glass windows. "It has the crest! Rose Strauss is a Thorndike!"

"You just made a big mistake," Frazier said.

Nancy reached for the door handle but Frazier grabbed her wrist and held it tight.

With his free hand he quickly reached into the glove compartment between the seats and pulled a dirty, ugly-smelling rag from a plastic bag. Then he powerfully clamped the rag over Nancy's face.

"Chloroform . . ." The word came from her lips and trailed off to a whisper as the world got farther and farther away.

The screeching of the car's front tires on asphalt was the last thing Nancy heard as she passed out.

Road noise woke Nancy up. It was the roar of tires on the road at high speeds. Her wrists hurt and so did her legs. This was the second time this creep had tied her up while she was unconscious!

She opened her eyes just a little. She was lying cramped in a C-shape in the backseat. Frazier was driving with one hand on the wheel and one hand gripping a car telephone.

He kept changing lanes in short, fast moves, bouncing Nancy all over the back of the car.

"I'm trying to keep up with them, but they know we're following," he said into the phone.

As Nancy's mind slowly began functioning again, she realized what Frazier was talking about. It must be George and Bess! He was following them. She wasn't sure where they were going, but she could make a good guess. They were probably on their way to Rose Strauss's house.

"Hey, look," Frazier said angrily into the car phone. "I kept the veil because I *wanted* to keep the veil, all right? Try going around in that circle for a while."

Nancy didn't want Frazier to know she was awake. She cautiously stretched her neck until

124

she could peek out the back window. They were on a highway—a fairly deserted highway. Behind them, six car lengths back, was the one car she didn't want to see: Cecelia's milky white limo with its LICORICE license plate.

"Look, sis," said Frazier. He changed lanes quickly again. "People think you're just a crazy, flaky nut. That's fine. But *I* grew up with you. I learned through experience to keep my back covered. You want to know why I didn't burn the veil? Because it's my insurance policy that you'll pay me what you owe me."

Nancy closed her eyes again and pretended to be asleep. But it was hard to keep her eyes closed when she heard what he said next.

"Sure, it's going to look just like an accident," Frazier said suddenly. "Three girls and an old lady driving around seeing the sights. Suddenly they misjudge a turn and drive off a cliff. Too bad. Trust me, sis. There won't be anything left when they're finished bouncing off the rocks."

Bouncing off the rocks. The words made Nancy shiver. These people were serious—dead serious. They weren't planning to scare her anymore. They were planning murder!

Frazier hung up the phone.

"Hey, Miss Detective," he said, looking at her in the rearview mirror. "Are you awake? You've worked so hard to mess everything up for us—but now it's our turn. And I don't want you to miss the fun."

"I'm awake," Nancy said. "Enough to know

125

that you're in big trouble. Assault, kidnapping, theft—those are just a few of the charges facing you."

"What are you? Some kind of lawyer?"

"I'm a lawyer's daughter, so I know," Nancy said. "Who do you think is going to fall the hardest? You or Cecelia?"

"You are," Frazier said with a big laugh. "Right off a cliff." He laughed so hard the car veered dangerously to the right. Nancy felt the tires leave the pavement and kick up stones from the shoulder of the road.

Then the car phone rang and Frazier had to straighten out the car before he could answer it.

"What do you want now, sis?" There was a moment of silence. "I'll tell you what we're talking about. We're talking about the weather, that's all," he said, laughing. "I *am* watching the road. Nice talking to you." He slammed the phone down, then popped a cassette into the tape player and turned up the volume.

The rest of the trip to Rose Strauss's house in Kennebunkport, Maine, was made with no further conversation. Ahead of them in the rented car were Bess and George, and behind them was the milky white limo—all three cars in a row, speeding after each other.

When she felt the car getting off the highway, Nancy struggled to sit up so she could see the digital clock on the car radio. More than two hours had passed since they had left Boston. Frazier was sticking closer to George and Bess now. Eventually Bess turned into a tree-lined street of small houses and slowed down.

At the end of the road, Nancy saw a cedar house with boards stained dark brown. The long driveway sloped and curved down toward the house, which was set back from the road. When Bess turned into the driveway, she pulled out of Nancy's sight. Tall pine trees all around obscured Nancy's view.

Frazier waited at the mouth of the driveway a moment, and Nancy could only imagine the action. George and Bess were probably jumping from the car. Then they would run to the front door and ring the bell.

If she was home, Rose Strauss would let them in.

A few minutes later Frazier steered the car into the driveway and coasted to a stop. "Well, looks like this little tea party is just about over," he said to Nancy as he got out.

There was no question about what Frazier meant. If she couldn't get out of the car and get help soon, she would be dead. No—that wasn't a fair way to put it. Bess, George, and Rose Strauss would be dead, too.

Think quick, Nancy said to herself.

Then she heard other car doors open and close.

"Frazier."

Nancy recognized Cecelia's voice, calling to her brother from behind.

"Leave car windows open a crack in warm

127

weather. Don't forget: Pets have to breathe, too."
Cecelia looked in at Nancy and smiled. It wasn't
the same innocent and warm smile it had been.
"Aren't you just as sorry as I am that you ever left
River Heights?"

"Come on, Cecelia. Time is money," said another voice. Nancy knew that voice, too. She
turned to the other side and saw the calm,
confident face of Jason Moss!

"I'm having second thoughts, Jason," Cecelia
said, watching sadly as Nancy squirmed against
her ropes.

"About what?" Jason asked with surprise.

"The windows. Close them up tight and lock
the doors, Frazier," Cecelia said. "It won't do us
any good to have someone hear her scream."

Frazier did what he was told, and through the
closed windows Nancy heard Cecelia say, "Well,
we have the veil, and we have a hostage. I think
we're ready to pay a visit."

# 15

## The Grandmother of the Bride

As soon as the threesome vanished from view, Nancy set to work. She was determined to stop them from hurting anyone. She managed to loosen the ropes tied around her wrists and ankles, but she was still stuck in the backseat of Frazier's car. So she started to rock back and forth, back and forth, moving toward the front of the car. She twisted and climbed onto her knees and pressed her face close against the car window. Then, with her teeth, she lifted the door lock button. It hurt her mouth to do it, but she pressed her lips around the door handle and gently pulled. At last the door swung open and Nancy climbed out, onto the ground.

She looked up into a face hovering over her. It was George.

"I went straight in the front and out the back door, before Cecelia and Jason came in. I had Bess tell them I'd gotten carsick and had to lie down," George said, explaining her appearance as she untied Nancy's ropes. "We knew they

129

were following us the whole way. Where did Frazier learn to drive, anyway? In a video arcade?"

Nancy shook the blood back into her hands and feet. "Quick," she said. "Hand me Frazier's car phone." Nancy dialed a familiar number and then heard a familiar voice.

"Lieutenant Flood speaking."

As quickly as she could, she told the lieutenant where she was and what was going on.

The lieutenant thought for a few seconds.

"This is risky, but I'm going to take a chance," Flood said. "I want you and your friend to go back in the house before anyone gets suspicious. That way you'll be able to stall until the police arrive. Keep the suspects talking for as long as you can.

"In the meantime I'll call the Kennebunkport police," Flood went on. "But I don't know how long it'll take them to get to you. Call me the minute it's over. I won't leave my desk."

Nancy thanked the lieutenant and hung up. Taking a deep breath, she and George marched into Rose Strauss's house. Under other circumstances the house might have seemed homey and quaint, but Nancy was too busy thinking about what lay ahead to look much at her surroundings.

"Anybody home?" Nancy asked, imitating Cecelia at the church.

"Nancy!" shouted Bess.

Nancy and George walked into a cozy living room. To Nancy's surprise, everyone inside was drinking hot tea. Bess and Rose Strauss sat stiffly on a couch, with Cecelia across from them in a straight-backed rocking chair. Jason Moss sat in an oversized chair which had room left over for one more person. Only Frazier was not sitting. He was pouring tea.

The veil sat in a heap on a round wooden table in the middle of the room.

The group looked startled to see Nancy and George in the doorway.

"Well, you're very good at attending parties you aren't invited to, aren't you, dear?" Cecelia said, regaining her composure. "My friend Greta thought you were most charming."

Rose Strauss remained silent.

"Now that we've gotten this little scare out of our systems," Cecelia said cheerfully, "let's get down to work." She leaned forward and looked directly at Rose Strauss. "Where is it?" Cecelia asked.

"I don't know what you're talking about," Rose said.

Nancy smiled. She knew Mrs. Strauss was being evasive—and she also suspected that the older woman could be very, very stubborn.

"What is she talking about, Nancy?" Bess asked quietly.

"Wait a minute, Cecelia," Nancy interrupted. "Mrs. Strauss, you have another piece of lace that goes with this veil, don't you?"

"Stay out of this, young woman," Rose said.

"You don't understand, Mrs. Strauss," Nancy

said. "My friends and I have been in this since the wedding. We've been chased, drugged, pushed, tied up, and threatened by these people. They are very dangerous, and I think you should tell them what they want to know."

"Or we could play your little game of Find the Bone," Jason said. "But in that case, you'd force us to search your house inch by inch."

The old woman sat for a moment. Then slowly she raised her cane and pointed it toward a dresser on the other side of the room. Frazier immediately started rummaging through it. In the back of the second drawer he found an old black leather box. Inside was another veil, exactly the same size and color as the one Cecelia had stolen from Meredith. But instead of a rose on the back, this veil had a ring of tulips, with stems intertwined tightly in the center.

Frazier tossed the second veil onto the table in the middle of the room.

Everyone leaned forward, intensely interested, as Nancy picked it up.

"These two veils are to be worn together, aren't they, Mrs. Strauss?" Nancy said. "I can see from these loose threads that they were once connected."

Nancy spread out the veil with the rose on the table. Its white folds fell gently to the floor. And then she lay the other veil over the top, so that the tulips encircled and nearly obliterated the rose underneath.

"That's the Thorndike crest!" Bess exclaimed. "Mrs. Strauss, where did you get that veil?"

"For goodness' sake," Cecelia snapped, "will everyone please stop calling her Mrs. Strauss?"

George and Bess looked at Nancy for an explanation.

"Mrs. Strauss has the veil," Nancy explained, "because she is really Rebecca Rose Thorndike."

"No," Rose said, breaking her silence. "I am *not* Rebecca Thorndike—not any longer—and I haven't been for years. I hated Brendan Thorndike. He was a cruel and selfish man. I divorced him and I didn't take a dime of his money. All I've ever wanted was never to have anything to do with him again."

Jason stirred his tea and said, "You took his children and he hated you for that."

"I saved *my* children," Rose said. "Look at that crest."

She walked over and looked down at the veils draped across the table and floor. "Look what happened to the single rose—*my* family. You can't see it. It's buried, practically swallowed up by the ring of tulips. That's what it was like to be married to him. I was just something else to stamp his crest on, that's all." She wrinkled the veils with a swipe of her cane and turned her back on them. "When I saw him teaching our children to love money more than people," she said, "I swore to myself I'd stop him. So I left and Robbie and Margaret grew up not knowing they were Thorndikes. They didn't need to. His money would only have caused them misery."

"Oh, what's a little misery when we're talking sixty million dollars," sniffed Cecelia.

"I don't understand something," Nancy said. "If you never wanted to have anything to do with Brendan Thorndike, why did you live so close by?"

"We didn't, at first," explained Rose, sitting down on the couch again. "After I took the children, I changed my name to Strauss and we lived in Europe for years. When I knew Brendan had given up looking for us, we came back and settled here in Maine, because I love this area."

Jason interrupted. "The truth is you loved living right under his nose when he didn't know about it. But *I've* known about you for years. I knew exactly where you lived."

"If you did, why didn't you tell Mr. Thorndike?" asked Bess.

"Why should I have?" Jason said. "The last thing she wanted was to be discovered by the old man. And that's the last thing I wanted, too. I was counting on her silence."

"Jason had gotten Brendan to rewrite his will so that we'd inherit the Thorndike money," Cecelia said. "It would have ruined everything for an heir to be discovered."

Rose wasn't listening. Her eyes glistened as private memories came back to her. "Robbie died suddenly at college, and then I had only Margaret," she said, holding a velvet pillow as if

134

it were a child. "Sweet, gentle Margaret. She married Jake Brody and they had a wonderful baby girl, Meredith. Then that terrible plane crash. I don't understand why you people don't see that life has enough pain without having to hurt people for money."

"Frankly," said Cecelia, "I think life without money is a pain."

Rose shook her head sadly.

"Meredith doesn't know anything about this?" asked George.

"No, I raised my grandchild the same way I raised my children—to be free, independent, confident in themselves, not in their name."

"Now I have a question for you, Rebecca," Cecelia said. "If you didn't plan to tell Meredith about her inheritance, why did you give her the veil and cause me all this nasty trouble?"

"I didn't want to give it to her," Rose said. "I kept the two layers of the veil separate and hidden for years. But Meredith found the rose veil one day when she was packing her things to move out after the wedding. She loved it and begged and begged me to allow her to wear it—especially when she found out I had worn it myself."

"And when you saw the photo of Meredith in the newspaper," Nancy said to Cecelia, "you started to worry."

"All this talk," Frazier mumbled to himself.

"Be patient, Frazier," Cecelia said. She took a sip of tea.

*Yes, be patient, Frazier,* Nancy thought to herself. *Because otherwise the police may not get here in time.*

"I saw the photo of Meredith in the paper," Cecelia went on, "and I said to myself, hmmm, that looks much too much like the Thorndike veil. I'd seen Brendan's wedding pictures, you see. And I didn't know that Rebecca had separated the two layers. Well, I said to myself, a nice, innocent, uninformed girl like Meredith shouldn't be walking down church aisles wearing something like that. You know how people like to talk. I was afraid someone might photograph it, or tell her that her veil looked just an itsy bit like the Thorndike crest."

"And then Meredith would have asked Rose, and Rose might have told her the truth," Nancy said.

"You just can't trust anyone to lie when you need them to," Cecelia said glibly. "So my little brother and I thought and thought and finally came up with a scheme to steal the veil so Meredith would not have to be bothered by all that gossip. Of course, Frazier was supposed to destroy the veil. And if he had done what he was told to do, we wouldn't be discussing this right now."

"But you're the head of all of Thorndike's companies now," Bess said to Jason. "You must be rich. Why do you want to take what belongs to Meredith? It's not fair," Bess said.

"I'll tell you what's not fair," Jason Moss said,

136

bolting from his chair and losing his composure for the first time. "In five days you have ruined what took me twenty years to set up. Twenty years of saying yes to that mean old man. Twenty years of doing his dirty work. Twenty years of jumping when he said jump. And you ruined it all—that's what's not fair. And that's why you're going to pay, and I don't care. I've worked too hard to let you stop me."

"Frazier, dear," said Cecelia, setting down her cup of tea, "once Jason catches his breath, I think it's time for you to explain the rules of the game."

Frazier stepped to the middle of the room.

"We're going for a little drive down the rocky Maine coast. You, you, you, and you," he said, pointing to Rose, Nancy, Bess, and George. "I will be your driver—but only up to a certain point."

Rose's face showed no emotion at all, but Bess and George looked confused.

Nancy finished his speech impatiently. "He means he's going to drive us over a cliff and jump out at the last second," she said.

Bess grabbed George's hand.

"Nancy Drew is annoying and provoking," Cecelia told her brother. "But don't let her lure you into a lengthy argument. We've taken all the time we can."

Jason nodded. "Let's go."

"I think there's something you should know," Nancy said. "Before I came in I called the police. They should be here by now. It will be better for

137

you if you give up." With all her heart, Nancy hoped that what she said was true.

"Let's find out," Cecelia said, opening the door and pushing Nancy and the girls out first.

Nancy looked all around the driveway and blinked twice. There were no police cars anywhere in sight. There were no police officers, either. She couldn't believe it, but it was true. Her stall hadn't worked, and without any help in sight she and her friends and Rose Strauss were about to be driven over the edge of a rocky cliff!

# 16

## *Reunion*

Nancy watched numbly as Jason tossed the veils in the trunk of the white limo and then hopped behind the wheel. She couldn't figure out what had happened. They'd given the police plenty of time to arrive, so why weren't they here?

Cecelia shot Nancy a triumphant smile, then climbed into the silver car. And Frazier pointed a gun at Nancy and the others, motioning them toward the rental car.

"I want *you* to drive," Frazier said, poking Nancy in the back. "Your friends and the old woman can sit in back. And don't forget, every-body, buckle up for safety."

"You know I told the police all about you," Nancy said, still stalling for time.

"I'm not worried about the police," Frazier said. "And when you're just a splatter on a rock, I won't worry about you, either."

He jabbed her with the gun and jerked his head toward Bess and George. "Hurry up," he told them.

Obediently Bess climbed into the backseat. But George and Rose hesitated. Nancy could tell they were looking for an escape route.

"Now!" Frazier screamed, yanking the older woman by the arm.

With dignity, Rose Strauss lowered herself into the car, and George followed.

Nancy looked around. Still no sign of the police. Finally she gave up and took her place behind the steering wheel. Once all of his victims were in the car, Frazier got in on the passenger's side of the front seat.

"Start the car," he said, putting his gun away and handing Nancy a set of keys.

Nancy drew the key up toward the ignition and hesitated before inserting it.

"I said, start the car!" Frazier was so tense he was beginning to lose whatever control he had had. There was a razor's edge to his voice.

Nancy slowly fit the key into the ignition and turned it.

But nothing happened.

"It won't start," Nancy said in a low tone.

Frazier pushed her hand away and tried the ignition himself. But the engine didn't make a sound.

"Rotten rental cars!" he shouted out the window at Cecelia. "It won't start."

Cecelia shouted back, "Mine won't either!"

"None of them will!" called Jason.

"Get out of the cars with your hands in the

air!" said a stern voice through a megaphone. The voice seemed to come from everywhere. "This is the police. You are surrounded. If you have any weapons, throw them on the ground!"

Nancy froze as she saw Frazier begin to reach for his gun.

"Get out of the cars," the megaphone voice commanded again.

Slowly the door to the silver car opened and Cecelia came out, looking around for the unseen police. Then Jason Moss stepped out of the white limo. He kicked the tire angrily—a little too angrily, because he hurt his foot. But he raised his hands in the air.

Meanwhile, however, Frazier stayed where he was. From her seat next to him Nancy could see clearly that Frazier was still going for his gun—and she was right in the line of fire. Just as his hand reached his belt, Nancy ducked. She held her head, waiting for the sound of gunfire.

Then a voice cried out, "Frazier, don't do anything stupid!" It was Cecelia.

Frazier looked at his sister and, as usual, did exactly what she told him. He climbed out of the car and dropped his gun on the ground.

After that, a dozen uniformed police officers moved quickly from their hiding places behind trees and bushes and large plastic trash cans. Squad cars and police vans roared down the street. Suddenly the whole neighborhood seemed to explode with activity.

The officer in charge rushed up to Nancy's car and looked in. "Is everyone all right?" he asked.

"No one is hurt, if that's what you mean," Rose Strauss said. "But I think it will be some time before we're all right."

"Yes, ma'am," said the policeman. "Which one of you is Nancy Drew?"

"I am," Nancy said.

"Come with me. I've got a Lieutenant Flood, Boston P.D., on a direct radio link," said the policeman.

As Nancy walked quickly to keep up with the officer, she asked why the police had remained hidden—and why the cars wouldn't start.

"Our mission strategy was to render the vehicles inoperable," he said in an official voice. "So before you came out of the house, we removed the rotors from the engines to prevent them from starting. We've found that if escape is not possible, most suspects become completely cooperative. Luckily, that's how it turned out."

He pulled a small piece of metal from his pants pocket. "This is the rotor blade to your rental car," he explained. It looked like the small blade to a toy helicopter.

While Nancy was still admiring their strategy, another officer handed her a radio microphone. She filled Lieutenant Flood in on all the details of the case.

"So it looks as though Meredith Brody is the Thorndike heiress," Nancy concluded.

"I'll try to keep this quiet," Flood said. "But I can't promise you that the newspapers won't get a hold of it. There are always a few reporters hanging around here, day and night."

"Meredith doesn't even know yet," Nancy told him.

"Well, you and her grandmother had better be here to meet her when she gets off the plane," Flood said. "She's going to need all the help she can get."

That night Rose called Meredith in Bermuda and told her to come home. And the next morning, Nancy, George, Bess, and Rose drove back to Boston to meet Meredith at the airport.

When Nancy and her friends arrived, Logan Airport was in chaos. Just as Lieutenant Flood had predicted, the Boston newspapers had printed the whole story—or at least as much of it as they knew. Nancy wondered whether Meredith herself knew as much about her new inheritance as all of these people did. Lawyers, police officers, reporters and camera crews, politicians, and well-wishers with signs filled the terminal. It was a major media event.

Lieutenant Flood, who was in charge of Meredith's arrival, met Nancy by the main entrance. He sent Rose, Bess, and George in one direction with his assistant. Then he and Nancy plunged through the main terminal and talked as they walked. Flood used his size to help them get through the noisy crowd, and his badge to get them through security.

"I've arranged a meeting room here in the airport," Flood said loudly as they walked through the crowd. "Oh, by the way, we found a red wig in Cecelia Bancroft's closet early this morning."

"I knew you would," said Nancy. "She wore it when she pretended to be the minister's wife, right?"

"Of course she had an explanation for the wig," Lieutenant Flood said. "But to tell you the truth, Nancy, no one at the precinct can understand half the things she says. For a while she almost had us believing the wig belonged to her dog. I think her bulb is loose in its socket."

Nancy had to laugh. Of all the people Nancy ever had caught, she would always remember Cecelia as one of the cruelest but also one of the most fascinating.

"Meanwhile, Frazier cracked like a rotten egg, too. He's admitted to everything—chasing you from the airport, pushing you off the Tea Party ship, slipping the knockout drug into your drinks at the Laugh Riot. The only thing he didn't do for his sister was send you that phony veil. Cecelia did that herself."

Suddenly Lieutenant Flood winced and he reached quickly for his ear. Nancy knew that meant someone was squawking too loudly in Flood's radio earpiece.

"Plane's landed," Flood said, grabbing Nancy's arm and hurrying with her toward the gate. "Keep the crowds back, boys!"

The police pushed one way but the crowds pushed the other. In the middle of the shoving tug-of-war, Nancy began to feel like a football player in a rough-and-tumble Saturday afternoon game. But with Lieutenant Flood blocking for her, she finally reached the doorway to the gate.

Everyone waited, watching the empty jetway. Five more minutes passed. Finally Meredith and Mark stepped into the terminal.

Camera lights blazed, strobe lights popped, and the mob of reporters shouted and called out questions all at once.

"Did you ever meet your grandfather?"

"Do you feel different being rich?"

"I don't know, I don't know," Meredith said, looking frightened.

Lieutenant Flood and his men quickly formed a protective circle around Mark and Meredith and tried to move them through the crowd.

Meredith was looking all around in confusion. When she saw Nancy standing just behind Lieutenant Flood, she pulled her into the circle and hugged her.

"How's Grandmother Rose?" Meredith asked.

"She's tired," Nancy said. "And she's a little afraid to face you."

"What are you going to do with the money?" shouted the reporters.

It was hard for Nancy and Meredith to talk. They were being pushed and pulled this way and that and shouted at from all sides.

"Congratulations, Meredith!" "Welcome home, Meredith!" people screamed.

With Flood leading the way, Meredith, Mark, and Nancy finally reached the meeting room, where Rose Strauss was waiting with George and Bess. George gave the newlyweds a big hug and welcomed them home.

At first, everyone stood in silence. Meredith stepped up to her grandmother. She seemed to want to hug her, but she hesitated. It was as though they were looking at each other over a wall.

"Is it true, Grandmother?" Meredith asked. "Why didn't you tell me before all this?"

"It's true," Rose said quietly. "I know what you're thinking. I know that you're angry with me, Merry, but I had very good reasons. You didn't know Brendan Thorndike. I believed I had to keep my children away from him and away from his money."

"Did my mother know?" Meredith asked.

"No," Rose said. "I never told my children."

"But he was my grandfather," Meredith said. "You should have told me."

"You didn't need his money, Merry, or all the pain he inflicted with it."

"You taught me to be stronger than that," Meredith said. "You should have trusted me to

146

decide about him for myself. Don't you know who I am?"

Tears formed in both women's eyes.

"You're right. I can see that you aren't afraid the way I was," Rose said. "You're right. I'm sorry I didn't tell you, Merry."

They were silent again. Then, at last, Meredith and her grandmother hugged and cried.

"The astrologer said if I didn't find what was stolen, my marriage would remain under a cloud of bad luck," Meredith said with a laugh. "She's going to have a heart attack when she reads the paper!"

"Well, you can thank Nancy Drew for this," Lieutenant Flood said. "I always thought her dad was a sharp cookie. You know, I knew this kid when she couldn't even feed herself with a spoon."

"Please, Lieutenant," Nancy said, blushing deeply.

"He's right," Meredith said, walking over to take Nancy's hands. "I have so many things to thank you for."

Nancy smiled to herself. She had started out looking for a missing veil and, in the end, had found a missing heiress as well. She was glad that she had been able to help Meredith. But solving the mystery and stopping Jason Moss from stealing a fortune had its own private rewards. That made Nancy feel even happier.

"You know, Meredith," Nancy said, "there is

147

one thing about this case I never figured out—Tony Fiske. Do you think he was working with Cecelia Bancroft?"

Meredith shook her head. "No, Tony didn't steal my veil. But he thought he could make some money from it."

"How do you know?" asked George.

"We ran into Tony in Bermuda," Mark said. "He tried to pick a fight with me in the hotel restaurant and landed in jail."

"Of course he didn't have any money, so he had to call us to bail him out," Meredith said. "He said he came to the wedding to cause trouble, but by accident he saw who stole my veil. He said the woman had already given him five thousand dollars to keep quiet. But for ten thousand he'd tell us who she was."

"We didn't believe him, of course," said Mark.

"For once he was telling the truth," Nancy said. "He did know."

"Well, Mrs. Brody-Webb," said Lieutenant Flood, "I think my men have held off the reporters as long as they can."

Meredith nodded and squeezed her grandmother's hand. "You'll stay with me, won't you, Grandmother?" she said. "I'm sure they'll want to talk to you too, since you've been a missing person for forty years."

"I will, but I don't have a thing to say to those reporters," Rose said. Obviously her old fighting spirit had returned.

"And Nancy, too," Mark said.

"Thanks, but no thanks," said Nancy. "We'll watch."

Nancy and her friends watched from the background as Meredith and her grandmother, surrounded by Mark Webb, Lieutenant Flood and some of his officers, answered questions from the press.

Then suddenly Nancy felt someone standing behind her.

"Hello," said the man with the flat voice and shiny summer suit.

"Hello, Harry Knox, Private Investigator," Nancy said, smiling and shaking his hand.

"My old pal, Flood, has been telling me all about this veil case you solved," Harry Knox said. "A neat piece of business. You're good. You're really good."

"Thanks," Nancy said. "But what are you doing here?"

"Well, I've never seen sixty million dollars in a size ten dress before," Harry said, his eyes scanning the crowd out of habit.

"I don't believe Meredith's a size ten," Bess said.

"Believe me, Bess," Nancy said, "if Harry Knox says she's a size ten, she's a size ten."

"Besides, I wanted to talk to you," Harry said. "You know, you should have told me you were a detective that day on the Tea Party ship."

"It didn't seem important," Nancy said.

"I've been hearing a lot of good things about you from Flood," Harry said. "I was thinking,

ness is good—of course our kind of
is always is. And I thought maybe you'd
to stay in Boston and put your name on my
office door. I could use a partner."

Nancy thought for a moment about what it
would be like to leave River Heights, to move to
Boston and be a professional private detective.

"Thanks, but no thanks, Harry," Nancy said.
"I'm not ready to move. And besides . . ." Nancy
put her arms around Bess and George. "I already
have two partners. And I wouldn't trade them for
anything in the world."